AF407093

Noah's Ark

Maebel Credence

Published by Maebel Credence, 2023.

This is a work of fiction. Similarities to real people, places, or events are entirely coincidental.

NOAH'S ARK

First edition. November 7, 2023.

Copyright © 2023 Maebel Credence.

ISBN: 979-8223648109

Written by Maebel Credence.

Table of Contents

A Gift

I twirled the diamond ring on my finger as my glare bore into the short brunette Marshal spoke to from across the room. We were supposed to be celebrating my birthday early since he would spend the next few days on a trip with his friends, but he seemed to be celebrating himself. If I were to speak to a man at one of Colette's parties, Marshal would seethe and call me a slut. Yet I had to watch as a tipsy stranger tugged her long hair flirtatiously, occasionally letting her hand fall over her cleavage when she laughed at something he said.

The moment her eyes met mine, my gaze shifted to a tall woman in all black sauntering in the door. I only ever saw Raven at Colette's, but we never spoke beyond a *hi* or *bye*. Most of our encounters, she cast more than a few glances my way. Even I couldn't hold the dominant gaze of the seductive woman in skintight clothing.

Three-inch stilettos made her over six feet tall, dwarfing Marshal, who always bore a sneer at the sight of her. He couldn't stand outspoken women, and she had no problem making him feel puny—even though he would never admit to it. Once, she'd grabbed him by his hair and slammed him against the wall, telling him he'd make for a *good little bitch*. I felt more than a little excitement at the thought of what he would do if he turned around and saw her towering above the few people who separated them.

Tonight, Raven had a petite redhead at her side. I never understood how the woman chose her partners, or what drew them to her. Maybe it was the sexy, tattooed bad girl vibe. *Madame*, the dainty girls always called her.

Forefinger hooked in the ring of the smaller girl's collar; Raven pulled her close for a kiss. The red-head's eyes twinkled with excitement. What I wouldn't give for Marshal to make me feel desired like that—minus the collar.

The brunette speaking to Marshal laughed, drawing my attention to her playful pat on his chest. The last time I acknowledged this behavior, he'd slapped me the moment we stepped out the door. The time before that, when I'd cried publicly, he'd berated and humiliated me.

No, it wasn't worth the confrontation.

"Elizabeth," Colette's soft voice called from behind me. At least I had a reason to turn from the sight of my jerk fiancée and the drunk brunette. But I couldn't blame her, she didn't know about me.

I went to the hall and caught sight of my best friend's head poking out a doorway. Her beaming smile gave away her excitement. At least, until she looked down at my incessant twirling of the ring. I hadn't told her about the engagement. I knew what she would say, and I always felt like a coward for my excuses not to leave.

But she didn't say anything aside from, "Happy birthday." She squeezed me in a long hug before reaching back to her dresser to a small white gift box.

I took it and untied the pink bow. I gently opened it and unwrapped the tissue to reveal five silver bands. Each had a ring connecting the front, and in that ring dangled a jasmine-shaped charm. Its milky opal petals shimmered as they swung. One was neck sized, so the others must have been matching bracelets.

"Thanks." I stroked the new gifts, admiring the play of light against the opal. It was too expensive of a gift for her to buy me. "You shouldn't have."

"Raven helped out. She got a discount for the set at work."

"Really?" I had trouble believing Raven knew my name, much less that she worked at a jewelry store. And for someone with her taste for black leather, it was so dainty and pretty. Even if they both split the cost, it would have been too expensive for a college student.

"I..." *can't accept this.* The words didn't come, though. Instead, I looked down to my crummy engagement ring. Marshal could have afforded better, yet my own friend and an acquaintance had bought me something nicer. He would be livid at the sight of the expensive jewelry.

"You deserve it."

"I should thank Raven." I bit my lip.

"She said you can thank her by going here." Colette reached into the top of the box to a small, folded piece of peach-colored paper.

"Noah's Ark?" I studied the scribbled name as I took the page. "She's inviting me to church?" Beneath the name was an address and the words *ask for Jonah*.

"Does Raven look religious?"

Colette had a point. God would smite her on sight, given her worldly ways.

"She said they gave her a place to stay and a job—a good-paying job. It's where she met Pris. They both had partners like..."

I sighed. Now I knew where this was going.

She continued, "I know Marshal is leaving for a few days, so I can help you pack." Her attention went to the small, pink scar on my cheekbone for far too long.

I twirled the ring on my finger, feeling Colette's stare on me. "He's getting better," I lied.

"He humiliates you."

A huff came from behind. "And not in a kinky way." I turned to see Raven with Pris at her side.

Red-cheeked from shame, I gave her a small smile. "Thank you, Raven, for the gift."

Her hazel eyes twinkled as they roved over me. But it wasn't sexual. There was something genuine to her look, maybe caring. I had to tilt upward to her face as she drew near and took the necklace from the box, though the intensity of her stare had me looking downward. She took a moment to connect the back. "You don't need to take anything with you to Noah's Ark—" She took another piece of the set and placed it on my wrist. "Jonah gets off at 3. And my god is he hot." So, it was a setup for a new guy to date.

"I appreciate this, but Marshal…" I sighed.

As she placed the second bracelet to my other wrist, she said, "He's getting to know that brunette fairly well in the guest room."

My shamed swallow caught in my throat. I could feel the adrenaline building in my system. The time I discovered him cheating wasn't one I cared to experience a second time. And maybe she confused him with someone else. He and I had moved past his previous behaviors.

Raven lifted my thigh. I was too absorbed in my thoughts to respond or stop her. I felt out of body as I watched Pris take something from Raven, then one of the bands and knelt down so my ankle rested on her leg. She secured the jewelry to one ankle, then the other. "You and Pris are a lot alike. Two months ago, she was with someone more abusive than Marshal."

I nodded, still only half there and half hung on the thought of my fiancée in a room fucking a stranger.

Raven curled a finger in the hoop in Pris's collar and pulled her close so their faces touched. "Good girl."

The petite ginger beamed. "Thank you, Madame."

As the two kissed, I turned my attention to one of the dainty bracelets and stroked the opal bloom. "I want to see him," I finally muttered.

Colette started, "Liz—"

I didn't let her finish before I stepped around her and out into the hall. Everyone I passed felt like one more person who knew Marshal's secret. One more witness if I unleashed the building tension. I couldn't even have men as contacts in my phone due to his jealousy. Yet I had never cheated on him.

Whatever Colette attempted to say to stop me went ignored. I opened the door to get a solid view of Marshal's pale ass as he pounded into the girl bent over the bed. They hadn't bothered moving the cardigans or purses, aside from the few that had fallen.

I found myself hoping he'd used a condom, so I wouldn't also be receiving a STI. Yet, I felt too out of touch with the situation to do anything. The hold on my arm felt nice. So dominant, yet gentle. *Raven.*

Colette snuck behind the grunting couple and plucked my pink clutch from near Marshal's boot.

Raven pulled me back into the hall before quietly closing the door. "Looks like he found a ride home." She removed the phone from my purse. "I'm mapping you to Noah's Ark." Once it was on the screen, she handed me the phone along with the peach sheet of paper.

By the time I'd reached the outskirts of the suburb, the shock of the situation had subsided. Not only had I left Marshal at Colette's, but I took his truck. I had half a mind to ram it over a few curbs or buy a baseball bat and go Carrie Underwood on it.

The maps app shamingly informed me I'd passed my turn. I slowed through the drizzle of rain in search of a paved road and, after about five minutes of searching, came to a building about as large as a Walmart Supercenter. There were no lights to draw attention to it, aside from a small one at a corner entry. I parked at the far end of the lot and attempted to remove the new jewelry. It didn't budge. After spending a good fifteen minutes fumbling with it, I gave up.

My phone buzzed. Forty-seven notifications from Marshal. Texts, calls, messages. What a nightmare this would be if Jonah refused to help me. I shoved the phone into my clutch before walking the moderately full parking lot.

As I drew nearer, hungry eyes trailed me. Most were towering males in black leather, and a few had scantily clad women at their sides. Some of those women wore black face coverings for a masquerade. I swallowed. This couldn't possibly have been the right place. Raven may have shared some fashion with these people in all-black attire, but this wasn't where she would have sent me.

"You, Bo Peep," a large man at the head of the line said. I had no doubt the insult was directed toward me given my flowy swoop-neck pink dress. "Come here." Despite his rudeness, it was an order I felt inclined to obey.

I arrived in front of him and noticed his leather bracelets with metal clasps and chains. When my mouth opened to speak, he halted me with a hand up.

"They're going to eat you alive in that pink dress. Who invited you?"

Blood drained from my face as I realized what I was doing. I left Marshal. Stole his truck. He would be livid.

I stepped backward, catching my heel in a crack in the pavement. The large doorman grabbed my arm, saving me from an embarrassing fall. A sign, perhaps. I couldn't turn back. I couldn't go back to Marshal. I had to find Noah's Ark.

I forced myself to stand straighter on my heels and removed the peach page from my purse. "I'm looking for a place called Noah's Ark."

One side of the man's mouth lifted in an unnerving smile as he took the paper. He held a hand to a bud in his ear. "Hey Noah, we've got a little lamb out here looking for Jonah." His tone held the mocking humor that had me deflate more every second.

I scowled at the prick, but knew better than to offend him. Did he think it was easy to go waltzing up to a strange place in hope of help? Was this a place of refuge?

Within a moment, the metal door behind him screeched open, and an unbelievably handsome man in a suit stepped out. He looked as though he was walking toward a photo shoot. If this was Jonah, Raven hadn't lied about him being hot. She neglected to mention drool-worthy, though. He must have been over six-foot-three, and his blue eyes pierced through the darkness that engulfed my shallow shell.

"Should I call Jonah?" the doorman asked.

"*That* is not a job for Jonah." This must have been Noah.

The doorman chuckled; the ridiculous sort of laughter that made me feel microscopic. My trance faded at the scratchy sound as he handed the page to the man in the suit.

They were mocking me. I turned to leave. Maybe I could stay with Colette as I worked up the courage to figure things out.

"Do you want help or not?" The deep voice sent a chill through me. I could keep going. Ignore whoever spoke, but in the push and pull of my mind, I turned to face that commanding tone like a moth drawn to flame.

"I do."

"I need identification."

I took my driver's license from my clutch. The brush of his hand to mine sent a flutter through me. He kept that hold and raised my hand to inspect the bracelet. He may have been an unapproachable man, but that only made his touch more appealing.

"Get a disclaimer set up for Elizabeth to sign," he said to the doorman, who retrieved an iPad.

"Safe word?"

"Jasmine. Definitely jasmine." He released my hand. His chiseled features didn't soften, but there was some subtle intrigue that eased my nerves. "Don't forget that."

I nodded as I scrolled down the print, scanning the small words before I signed.

"Follow me."

As I passed the doorman, he said, "See ya later, little lamb." And that was what I felt like, a lamb stepping into a dark corridor where wolves may lay in wait. The loud reverberations of my steps made me cringe at the interruption to the silence.

"Are you Noah?" I asked. I attempted to soften my steps while also keeping pace with his long strides.

"To some people. Who referred you to Jonah?" he asked.

"Raven."

He stopped at a door to punch a keypad, casting me a sideways glance. "She would do that just to annoy me." Given my need for help, I couldn't respond to his claim of me being an annoyance. But it was better to be an annoyance to someone for a little while than to be Marshal's doormat.

The inside of the room looked nothing like the bland halls or outer building. He passed a fancy black leather chair to sit at the edge of a clean desk.

"What did Raven tell you about us?"

"That you provide a place for women to go." I twisted the ring on my finger. The nervous habit had him glance down at it.

"For what?"

Instead of waiting for his gaze to connect with mine, I examined the bookshelf on the far wall as I spoke. "To live."

"No wonder she recommended Jonah." He leaned back, then opened a drawer. "We train anyone in need of a job—" he had several pages in hand "—insurance, housing, food, training. You will start out at two to four K a month. Plus tips."

I wasn't an idiot. That wasn't the sort of job a person got from a simple training to help them off their feet. "What's the job?" Now I did watch him.

"That is up to you, Elizabeth." He purred my name, though there was still iciness to his tone. "Come here."

My feet obeyed the order before my mind seemed to will it. When I stood only a few feet in front of him, he held out a pen and a clipboard with paper on it.

"Sign this." His signature was already on the page.

I swallowed. "I don't know what I'm signing."

"Your consent to live and train here. My guarantee that you will possess the skills required for the job of your choosing. Most women start out as waitresses. We also have bartenders. Some go on to other tasks." He pressed the board to my hand.

I stepped back. "I'm not a prostitute."

"We operate by the law. There are no prostitutes." At the silence, he added, "Nor are there strippers or escorts. The training is forty days; less if you are a quick learner. Then you fulfill a three-month contract with whatever position you want. After that, you can stay or go. Most individuals we help choose to stay."

I nodded. A little over four months to get on my feet. I could do that. "Why forty days?"

"Because it's Noah's fucking Ark, not Jonah's whale ride." His sarcasm was softened with a smile that quickly faded.

I took the pen and paper from him and signed the document. After he collected it, he stood, chest against me. The smell of sandalwood tickled my nose before he took my hand and removed my engagement ring. After he slid it into his pocket, he pushed a wide banded, black ring on my finger.

"You only get one of these smart rings. You choose when you want to wear it. If anyone or anything bothers you, all you have to do is fist your hand and press your thumb on it to activate it. If we are apart, my phone will receive notification. If I'm nearby, I will also hear the sound it makes." When he squeezed my hand and pressed my thumb to the flat top of the ring. It buzzed loud and lit. "No one will bother you at that warning."

"So you know where I am at all times?" I asked.

"When you're wearing it." His gaze went to the band at my neck. With speed, he had a finger hooked in it and pulled. "I strongly urge you to keep it on until after your training is complete."

I couldn't pull away—and I wasn't certain I wanted to.

"Unless you are with me, halls and rooms are off limits. Most doors are one way, so I don't want you getting lost. You go where I tell you, when I tell you."

Too close. He was too close, yet I still didn't care to pull away. "Lesson number one, if this bothers you..." His hand went between my thighs. Too close to my panties, it went, yet I said nothing. If anything, my legs spread a bit as he stroked the fabric.

When I finally attempted to break away, he pulled the necklace tighter.

I pushed his arm downward, hugging my chest.

He hooked his hand around my thigh, spun, and had me laid on my back on the large desk. My struggle ceased from the fear and excitement of the strong man pinning me. "As I was saying. If this bothers you, all you have to do is fist your hand, so the pressure signals me or anyone else who behaves in a way that makes you uncomfortable."

But I made no fist, only stared up at him, panting from the closeness. No one, certainly not Marshal, had ever caused my body to respond the way Noah did. He'd turned my mind into pudding.

"Are you going to stop me or are you asking me to fuck you?" He wedged a knee between my legs and pressed his hips to mine. My mind whirred. I didn't know if he was a danger to escape or a pleasure to spread my legs wider for. When I didn't move, his hand raised to mine, forcing it to ball until the ring vibrated and buzzed. "You've got forty fucking days with me. I suggest you learn to use that ring, little lamb." When he raised, he readjusted his suit jacket. "Any questions?"

"Jonah. I was referred to meet Jonah." Raven had referred me to Jonah, not Noah. Now I understood why she wanted me to go to someone specifically.

"If you wanted Jonah, you should have signed his contract. Besides, he wouldn't even know how to appreciate the jewelry you're wearing."

What had Raven gifted me—or was it even a gift? Noah took my small purse from the leather chair. "You won't be needing any of these belongings any longer."

The clack of my heels was the only sound as I walked behind Noah in the wide corridor.

"We start tomorrow, but I will show you around." After he placed my clutch into a locker, we exited a door into a loud area that smelled of alcohol. The faces of the guests could be made out in the dim room.

"If you want, I can let you assist at the bar for a few hours a week." He slowed at the bar, where a short blonde beamed at him from her stool. "Jaimie, Elizabeth needs an outfit."

"Right away, Noah." When she stood and turned away, I got a good view of how skimpy the outfit would be. Her black halter hardly reached the bottom of her ribs, and the skirt wasn't appropriate for any business I'd visited. Unintentionally, my hand balled; the buzz hardly audible over the voices.

Noah glanced me up and down. "Is there a problem?"

"I...I don't want to wear one of those outfits."

"If you don't like anything she brings, you don't have to wear it."

I hadn't expected the kindness given his previous demeanor. My nerves calmed a bit. "Thank you."

He called to another woman and asked her to prepare a drink for me. As she scooped ice, I caught sight of the chain that dangled from a silver band around her neck—a band similar to mine. When she came to us, her lead had extended taut at its full length. Her head remained down when she pushed the drink to me. My gaze followed the chain to the other end of the bar, where it connected to a man in a suit. His glare remained on her, as though searching for fault.

Subconsciously, I felt the dangling jasmine on my neckpiece.

Noah spoke, "Raven oversaw her training; even gave her that pretty choker. I'm surprised she didn't take you under her wing."

It was a little comforting to hear Raven's name. But then again, Raven had gifted me something that appeared very similar to what kept that woman on a leash. I wanted to run, truly and without a doubt, I wanted to leave, but this wasn't worse than Marshal. He was worse than anything I'd seen here.

Jaimie returned with a bag in hand. "You're needed in the back," she told Noah.

"Watch her." He didn't even give me a glance when he left. I couldn't understand the man, who was both nice and abrasive.

The woman spread out several clothes for me to choose from. All were black, of course. Her voice was higher and softer than I expected. "I also found you some nicer ones, so you're dressed cute." She pulled a few items out.

"That's lingerie." I recoiled when she held out a see-through bra.

"Noah likes lace." She beamed at me. "How did you land him? He never trains anyone."

"I came for Jonah." I looked through the outfits of skirts and short tops to match.

"He doesn't train anyone either."

"Then what does he do?" Had I been sent for a job or a date? If Jonah didn't train, he must not have provided jobs. I took a long drink through the straw. The beverage tasted like straight alcohol with a slightly tart apple flavor.

She shrugged and nodded to someone behind me. "You could ask him yourself."

I turned, but only saw Noah. Annoyed, I turned back to Jaimie. Soon enough, he was by my side, glancing down at the outfits.

"I don't want to wear any of those," I said, immediately worried I might be kicked out.

"I wouldn't either." His smile reached his eyes.

I blushed at the sight, unable to force more action than a bite to my lower lip.

"What's your name?" he asked.

I glanced around to see who he spoke to with such a charming smile.

Jaimie giggled. "She's new. Noah brought her to pick up some clothes."

He laughed in response. "I'm Jonah. Cursed to be Noah's twin. He manages the people. I oversee operations." The tone of his voice made a dip land in my tummy. He was nicer and warmer.

"Elizabeth."

"You don't seem to fit the part to work the front."

Relief burst into me. He might help me to bypass whatever training Noah planned. "My friend sent me here to meet you." I took a long drink until air slurped into the straw. The pucker of my face brought another grin to his handsome features.

"Let's head to the back. You don't need to be corrupted by all this."

I hopped to my feet. Following his lead, I weaved through chattering people. The door we went into opened to a larger room with lights toward the middle. We stayed close to the wall as we moved through.

"Many of the doors are one way for safety. I'm sorry I have to bring you through here." It wasn't as loud, some talking, but the openness gave us distance from people toward the other side of the room.

I nodded as I kept up. When we were halfway through the large space, a loud pop rang out, followed by whistles and cheers. I stopped to see what the people were watching.

"Let's keep moving." His hand was to my lower back, guiding me forward. We were close to a door when a loud ruckus had me turn to the lit area. People cleared as two men scuffled.

"Shit, you go ahead and wait at the door under the exit sign."

But I couldn't take my eyes off the stage where a naked woman hugged a beam. No, she was bound to it with thick ropes.

A pop.

The sound had been a flogger a man in a suit used on her.

I couldn't move. All I could do was stare at the woman. She wasn't the only woman tied. Another lay on the floor, limbs bound by leather straps, spread in the shape of a star. The muscled man fucking her wasn't being gentle.

If this was what went on in the front, what went on in the back? It no longer felt like a better alternative to Marshal. More horror filled me as I saw the cages with people in them. But as I rushed toward the exit sign, a light flashed beside me. What I'd thought was a black wall was actually a window. A man stepped in, a woman on hands and knees at his side. A chain dangled down from his hand. I sped past to the man in a leather vest at the exit door.

"Jonah told me the exit was this way," I lied, but it was obvious I was headed toward the exit. A buzz and beep came from my fist, bringing me to the awareness of the ring Noah could track. Fuck that. I yanked the ring off. "I don't need this anymore."

The man smirked as he opened the door. "Thanks for coming." The way he spoke the words was laced with a tone of perversion.

Inside, I yanked off my heels to silence my steps and briskly strode the dim hall which forked, revealing doors. They had to be to the rooms like the one that lit up. I went straight toward another glowing exit sign. The hallway felt like an eternity before it turned to the right. More doors with windows that permitted me to see what looked like furniture designed for torture, human-sized cages, and restraints of metal or rope. And this was where Jonah planned to take me.

The next sign pointed to the left to a darker hall lit only by the stretch of light from a room and the glow of the distant, red sign that would lead to freedom. Finally! It felt as though I finally wasn't circling the club with its long, endless halls and right turns.

At the strip of light from a half-open door, I stopped and peered in on a smaller stage. A man hung from shackles attached to a device that resembled a cross. A full covering was on his head that tipped forward. Silent people stood by. One man had his dick out, stroking it. I had thought they only did these sick things to women.

Where was the person who'd caused the red slashes on his bruised back? The silence was unnerving.

I crept closer.

Loud steps inside preceded a woman dressed in a full-body leather suit. She made Raven look like a kitten. If she had done that to the man—

A soft noise came from behind.

I turned, foolishly ignoring the need to sneak away. Before I had seen the person, a hand was to my mouth, and an arm hooked around me so my arms couldn't raise in fight.

"You're a pretty thing," he whispered.

My struggles were in vain against the strength of the man who held firm and dragged my struggling body. He turned into the doorway to a blackened room. Hardly a strip of light extended into the room, lighting it enough so I could only see the hand that moved in front of me.

"If you scream, I will drag you out and share you. Understand?"

Head nodding with desperation, I whimpered into his palm. I had been so close to the door. So close to leaving. I would have if I hadn't stopped.

"Good little slave." His hand lowered.

"Please," I whispered. "I'm leaving the club."

"I'll let you go." Hands groped down my body, one dipping beneath the skirt of my dress. "Just as soon as I give you what you came for."

"Jonah told me to come here and wait for him." I squirmed at the touch.

A firm hand glid the length of my arm down to my hand, stroking my ring finger, then to my other hand. That ring. This man was waiting for a fucking buzz before he would back off.

"I took off my ring to leave. Just—"

"Don't speak," he growled while lifting my dress, slowing to graze over my bra. "Raise your arms." Fear of what would await disobedience had me willing to obey. Once the dress was off, he undid my bra at the clasp. Without a need to receive orders, my arms dropped to let the bra fall to my feet.

I attempted to cover my chest, though he pushed my arms away to grope my breasts.

His breath teased my ear as he spoke. "You lay in bed fantasizing about running down a dark hall or alley alone, hoping a man will drag you into darkness and overpower you as you fight."

Shameful to admit it, I had that fantasy. It was something I'd thought about on several occasions when I touched myself at night. But a fantasy is private. Fantasies were in the mind, not something to act out.

He pushed my chest to the cold wall before his hand slithered around to stroke into my panties, bringing an unwanted gasp to escape me. "You're drenched for a good fucking already."

"No." I shook my head.

"I told you not to speak." A ball pressed into my mouth, and he tightened its strap behind my head. The force stretched my jaw to discomfort. He didn't need to gag me, not unless he planned to cause me to scream. When I flailed to get free, he stepped against me so my whole body pressed to the wall. My responding cry went unheard.

Another bout of anger swept through me, but not at anyone else. I was angry with myself. I had broken Noah's rules, ignored the warnings, gotten myself into this situation. A cold tickle to my neck pulled me from my thoughts. The light scrape of metal sounded as a small chain went through the ring of the silver choker.

"Hands to your chest."

I obeyed, whimpering into my gag, only seeing the small bit of light that reflected on the chain. It snapped to one bracelet, then the other. Both connected to the circlet at my neck. His warm hands cupped my breasts, squeezing at my nipples. "I'll pierce and chain these once I get you in my dungeon." But he only acted this torment out. This was just some dark fetish I had gotten caught in. That was all. He was just saying things. He wouldn't take me anywhere, would he? No matter what my excuses were, it didn't make me feel any more certain.

Hushed voices accompanied steps in the hall.

"Should I let them join us?" he asked. "We all came to find the little lamb who wanted wolves to play with her."

I shook my head silently.

"Turn around and sit in the chair."

I turned. Soon after, a light came on above a seat that reclined. Dear god, it looked like a chair equipped with items medical professionals might use, including the hose and mouthpiece for nitrous oxide that my dentist had.

The door behind me snapped shut, and a bolt thudded. Locked.

He'd locked people out, or had he locked me in? All I could do was stare at the setup. Maybe this had been the wrong choice.

A whistle of air preceded a painful sting to my rear. I stumbled from the pain and spun to back away from him. Dark shadows swept his jaw and chin from the one light above the chair. But a dark, reflective mask covered too much of his face for me to ever identify him. He raised a riding crop. Had his face been visible, I feared it may be that of a demon. The crop whipped forward, landing on my slit.

"In the chair."

His order and where he stood with the ability to dole punishment offered no opportunity to escape him. My steps backward didn't stop until I bumped the seat and plopped on it.

"This is going to be so much fun, little slave." He set the crop on a tray beside the seat. "No wonder all our clients who are dentists choose this room."

I thought to all the stories of dentists drugging and sexually assaulting their patients, and this seemed like the layout for such fetishes to occur.

He leaned forward and guided my panties down my legs. For a moment, he only looked at my displayed slit, then he ordered, "Lift and spread them."

I obeyed, turning my face to the side so this man didn't see my reaction to what he was about to do.

He continued to guide my leg high enough to connect ankle to wrist. From the corner of my eye, I watched him lift another silver chain to the anklet. After securing the chain— which only gave a few inches of leeway—he connected the other ankle and wrist to each other. He pushed my hips wider apart, so I was more frog-like as I attempted to keep my ankles and wrists from pulling my neck. With little flexibility, I had no choice but to hold myself in that position.

But he didn't mount me as I thought he would. He pulled a tray from the tool table. A slosh of sprayed water preceded him swirling something beside me. All the while, my humiliation increased. That's what this was, a domination and humiliation fetish. Then the flash of silver caught my eye, a long straight razor. I jerked, rolling against the armrest that caught my fall. The fetish took on new meaning when blades were involved.

"I'm going to need you to hold still so I don't cut anything accidentally." His tone remained calm, as though he didn't hold a torture device near my exposed private parts.

A motor started beside me. Next came a clear nose and mouthpiece. I inhaled. Several times my shuddering lungs took in the sweet drug within. Calm. It made me feel too calm to react to him. The device lowered to a hook near my face.

"That's better; nice and calm. We're just trimming things up a little more." He moved me into position. Warmth tickled over my flesh on one side, slowly followed by the soft strokes of the razor. Any of his calming words or praise went ignored by me. Who the fuck drags someone into a room to do this? It certainly wasn't part of any fantasy I'd secretly had about being overpowered by a man.

He shaved me smooth between my legs and all the way to my rear. After he sprayed warm water to cleanse the area, he said, "That's better." The voice too calm and composed.

Warm fingers explored my entrance, responding to my body's quivering reaction to his touch. As they dipped inside, a loud swallow caught in my throat. This wasn't something I would let him receive satisfaction from. Deeper they went with ease from my wetness. The chains didn't permit me much movement, not unless I wanted the circlet to dig into the back of my neck. Now I had to hate Raven for locking the entrapping jewelry onto me.

In and out. His thumb joined, rubbing my nub that had already begun to respond. My hips cruelly betrayed me as they moved with the flow. My chest humiliated me as I panted, and my back arched to lean up to him as his splayed hand roved up my stomach to left breast and stopped over my racing heart before continuing upward to squeeze my neck. He leaned onto me heavily, so my legs and arms had to accommodate and spread for him. At the back of my head, the slow glide of his fingers stopped, and the gag loosened before he tossed it onto the floor.

The following kiss was slow, passionate, continuous as his fingers worked a magic I'd never experienced. An embarrassing moan escaped me. He hadn't given me this choice, nor did he give me freedom to welcome the touch. He wouldn't stop until—

"Cum for me."

I gasped when he hit the perfect spot. Walls tightening over his fingers, legs trembling, body spasming. It wasn't an orgasm I could describe; it was one I'd fought that came all the more powerful.

His torso lifted from me so he could unclasp his pants and pull out his cock. When his arms braced above my shoulders, he said, "Look at me as I ride you."

Without hesitation, my gaze landed on his, but it was too powerful. Despite my attempt to turn away, his strong forearms enclosed on either side of my face. It wasn't like I could see much, even his eyes were shrouded from the mask's shadow.

I waited for the sound of a condom wrapper, but he didn't bother.

He buried his massive cock into me. My widened eyes answered to the force that felt as though it was almost too big. Even if I'd wanted to, I couldn't claw at his back, nor could I wrap around him. All I could do was lay there, arms and legs unable to move from where his weight had pressed them at my sides. His arms released my head, and he lowered his lips to mine, locking together despite my body bouncing upward with every thrust.

"I'm going to chain you to my bed and rut you until you can't walk." The heat of those words sent excitement through me, imagining being bound to a bed and thoroughly used. I couldn't tell my body to ignore the feel of him when those thoughts came to mind.

Before I became aware of his intentions, he'd snapped the chains on my ankles. An exciting feeling flowed through me as he lifted my body to straddle his as he spun to sit on the chair. The pumping of his hips became even more intense when his mouth latched onto my breast.

He was about to cum inside me, and without protection. I struggled to break free, but he slammed me onto him, holding my waist as his seed blast into my walls. The steady rock of his pelvis sent me into a blissful climax to milk him of any remaining cum.

My eyes closed, and the side of my head slumped onto his shoulder. I didn't bother to see the mask that went to my face, sending another dose of nitrous oxide into me.

"I'm going to have so much fun with you."

It wasn't the gas that caused my weakness, but the lack of food and sleep as well as the strong drink I'd had. I didn't want to open my eyes as he lay me down on the chair.

Pounding in my head greeted me when I awoke. An amber glow lit a large room that appeared to be a mix between a bedroom and an office. I sat up weakly and pushed a red fleece blanket off before placing my foot on the dark carpet. I doubted the ache between my thighs would let me walk too far.

The haunting memories of a stranger in the darkness prodded at my mind. Someone had bound me and fucked me hard. And by my exhaustion, drugged me as well. I didn't even know who had dragged me into that freaky fetish room. Lucky for both of us, I had an IUD.

The door opened, brushing along carpet. I turned to see one of the twins. He removed his jacket, leaving him in a white shirt and black suit vest.

"You're awake." The handsome man strode the short distance to me. "Jonah." He must have known I was uncertain which brother he was. Even in my mood, I couldn't help but let my eyes rove over his toned body beneath the fitted clothing. Maybe it was his smile, or simply knowing he was the respectable brother. Then again, he attempted to lead me into the hall where I was attacked.

I curled the blanket around my shoulders and scooted away, wincing from the pressure between my legs. I looked down, spotting green socks with cherries peeking out from beneath the cuffs of his slacks. Aside from my pink dress, it was the only colorful clothing in this club. I felt myself. My dress was on, but not my bra.

The couch dipped beneath Jonah's weight as he sat beside me. His cool hand raised to press against my cheek before he stretched to an end-table and handed a glass to me. "Fruit Punch Gatorade. It'll cure any ache...or hangover." His smile had been the only comfort I'd had since arriving, yet overshadowed by whoever had thoroughly fucked me. It may have been amazing sex, I may have even brought it upon myself by removing that ring and entering that back hall, but it was no less humiliating to be in that position.

"How did I get here?" I asked as I took the drink. Curiously, I studied his response in case he attempted to deceive me. Not that I could tell if someone was lying, but I would try.

"Noah found you asleep in one of the back rooms." When I said nothing, he flashed a small grin. "I had worried you ran off once you saw the place. It isn't exactly somewhere I would bring a woman I wanted to keep around."

A humored huff escaped me. "I would hope you wouldn't tell her to go running around in those back halls."

Jonah groaned and leaned his elbows on his knees. "Noah fired the doorman when he learned you were allowed back there without escort. No one bothered you, did they?"

My heart fluttered at the consideration for me, but the humiliation of knowing I'd gotten lost and fucked tamped out any joy.

"No. I just got scared and hid when I heard people." I took a long drink, hoping to hide my deception behind the glass.

He sucked in through his teeth and nodded, but his smile returned as he sat up. "You were wanting a job..."

"No. I just want to go home." I stared into the ice in the glass. It was saddening to think of how nice Jonah was, but the possibility of what he may consider as a job for me didn't seem appealing.

"Oh." His voice was low. "It doesn't have to be a job in the club."

"Thanks, but I think I'll just go ahead and leave."

His face screwed in an exaggerated wince. "One of our patrons ran his truck into yours—well, I'm assuming an ex's."

My head slumped to my knees at the thought of Marshal's truck smashed. Life couldn't get any worse, but I felt too broken to cry. This was a mess, and all because I thought I deserved better than Marshal. Even if I accepted a job, it would be Jonah's pity for me.

"Just rest. I'll drive you wherever you need to go."

The door clicked, and a tall figure walked in. I jolted, not wanting to be near anyone from this seedy establishment. I looked up, realizing it was Noah.

Noah whispered something to his brother and handed him a glass with a red liquid in it.

"Right," Jonah said. He gave me the Gatorade Noah brought. "Have another. I need to take care of something. This shouldn't take too long." He snuck out, leaving me with Noah.

Noah's gentle grin wasn't near as charming as Jonah's. That was the only way they differed.

I drank quickly.

He came over and took the glass. "My brother is fond of you." He carried it to the large oak desk. "I think he would do just about anything for a date."

I looked down at my hands. Under other circumstances, Jonah may have been someone I liked, but I didn't want to spend another moment here.

"He wouldn't know what to do with a woman like you." Noah sat against the edge of the desk.

I understood well what he wanted, and I was more than happy to leave. I sat forward, aching from the movement.

He took off his suit jacket and crossed his arms over his broad chest. "You signed a contract to receive training from me, not to cuddle with Jonah." He leaned forward.

My hands began to tremble. Slowly, I scooted forward and stood. "I'm not interested in working here." An ache in my groin flared, and every barefoot step was heavier than the last. I didn't make it far before he grabbed me and shoved me face down to the desk.

"I didn't say you could leave." His arm was against my back, holding me in place as he wrapped a wide leather collar around my neck. "You haven't earned that choker you're wearing yet. It's for good slaves." The thought of Raven giving me the jewelry made me wonder if this was her intent. But she had mentioned Jonah, not this psychopath. His free hand snaked up my skirt, unhindered by panties. "You're even more excited for me than when I had you bound."

Just the realization Noah had been my attacker nauseated me. I was too weak to put up much of a struggle as his knee knocked my legs apart.

"This is assault."

"Then use the ring or say a safe word." He shimmied free of his pants.

I winced. "I don't have either."

"You received both." His large cock slammed into my sensitive cunt, knocking me forward. "I was beginning to miss how good you feel wrapped around me." He stilled as he reached forward and stroked the nub between my legs, bringing a moan from me.

"This was in the contract you signed." He cupped my left breast, stroking my sore nipple, then pulled on the collar, causing my back to arch. Something about the way he forced that hold had desire pulsing through me. A need between my legs had me slamming backward against him. His pounding was so fast, I couldn't get a grip on the table.

"I want you to cum for me!"

No. He had humiliated me and bound my wrists and ankles to my neck. Forced orgasms. Toyed with my body as though it was his. I shook my head. Not in a thousand years!

The collar yanked backward, hindering my breath and arching my back further. "You're not going to breathe until my cock is strangled by your pretty little cunt." His next pull of the collar further backward had overwhelming pleasure rush through me, and my walls milked his cock that slammed deep and pulsed into me. I fell forward as the collar slackened.

He rolled me onto my back, scanning my heated face as he spoke. "My doorman has already paid your home a visit, so your ex doesn't touch you. You are going to refuse Jonah's job offer, let him drive you home, then I am going to pick you up and you will fulfill your contract with me."

If he thought I would let him bring me back here so he could fuck me non-stop for months, then he would discover how wrong he was.

"Don't glare at me unless you want the crop." He unclasped the collar then leaned down to kiss me. The once rough and dominating man had become gentle—despite his threat. He hummed his approval against my lips. "Take a shower."

By the time I glanced to the bathroom, then back, he was gone, and the office door was closing. *Fucking mad man.*

Jonah's shower sprayed down like warm rain. Given the shocks I'd endured, this offered some comfort. The soap calmed me with a subtle coconut fragrance I'd caught on Jonah.

After drying off, I put on a plush white robe. A note was attached to the top drawer with "Elizabeth" written in neat cursive. I pulled it open, where every bath toiletry imaginable was waiting for me. Had he placed these after I was found? It was both sweet and creepy. No matter how kind, he did work in a fetish club, and that wasn't the type of man I wanted in my life.

I would need to disappear as soon as he dropped me off, and I wouldn't let him take me to my apartment, where Noah would find me. Jonah was nice enough I could trust him to drive me to Colette's, but she may contact Raven. Brushing through my long, brown hair, my gaze landed on a chair with a black dress and undergarments. My pink one was no longer in sight. I shivered at the thought of someone taking it and then leaving me with his preference of clothing to match the fashion of the weirdos here, but I wouldn't walk around without clothing. I hung the robe and slid on the lacy undergarments then wrapped myself in the short, silky dress before stepping out.

Seated at his desk, Jonah glanced up from typing on his phone. Dimples formed as he smiled and lowered it. "You look beautiful."

I blushed. No matter my opinion of his brother or the club he owned, he was handsome. My steps were slow as I attempted to hide the ache from everything Noah had done to me.

Jonah stood and came over, handing the phone to me. "It's a company phone for you."

"Thanks, but I just need a ride home."

"You don't even know about the job."

Being here felt like I didn't escape the life I wanted to leave behind, and I needed to get away before morning when Noah would be searching for me. He was the sort of man who kept his promises and could easily use the signed contract as a way to hold me in his dungeon against my will.

"Of course," Jonah muttered low from behind me. "Keep the phone in case you change your mind." It slid into my hand. His face moved to mine.

I winced at the memory of those same eyes looking down at me and kissing me in one of the back rooms.

He sighed as he backed away. "Then tell me where you want to go."

I gave him an address in my complex, but not my apartment number. Soon we were out the door with a bag containing my soiled dress. The ride in his sporty BMW was silent, aside from the soft leather grunting against my thighs as I repeatedly readjusted.

When we turned onto a road with potholes, his hand landed on my leg, strong and firm gripped. Before this point, he'd seemed so gentle. At my whimper, he stroked down to my knee. We were less than a minute from the apartments when the car began to creep.

"Thank you," I said, appreciative of the ride.

"I just think..." He pulled into my complex.

I pointed. "Mine is there."

His tone turned icy. "No, it isn't." He knew that wasn't the one I lived in. I couldn't hide my fear from him, nor could I hold his stare.

He parked, facing the dark field away from the buildings.

Slowly, I lifted the door handle—locked.

"I can walk from here."

"I believe it would be in both our interests if you accept a job from me." He reached into the center console. "Whatever you want to do."

Like be his live-in whore? "Thank you, Jonah, but..."

He pulled a small bottle and tipped it downward.

My mind raced at the thought of being drugged once more. I jerked harder at the door, unthinking of a need to fight him until he leaned to me. He grabbed my head and forced a damp cloth that muffled any cry as I struggled.

There was a coldness in his hold. "It's clear you aren't responsible enough to make decisions for yourself."

I held my breath as I twisted. He pulled my head under his arm, pinning it as he put the car in gear. No matter how hard I tried, my body weakened, and vision darkened.

• • • •

WE WERE ON THE ROAD when I regained consciousness. There was a hint of lightness in the sky, but the oncoming cars felt as though their high beams were on. My hands were bound in rope when I tried to wiggle free.

"Please don't resist."

I leaned against the window as I looked at Jonah, half wondering if he had been Noah all along. Noah would probably have turned it into a sick game, though. And there was a bit of remorse to Jonah's expression as his eyes flicked from the road to me.

My mouth felt sticky when I spoke. "What the fuck is wrong with you?"

He jerked the gear to shift as he zipped into the fast lane. "We have plenty of time to overcome this, so please refrain from saying things you may regret."

"Like calling you a psychopathic rapist?"

A muscle in his jaw ticked. "I've never raped anyone." He reached for my leg.

I swiped at him with my bound arms. "So, it's not considered rape if they're in your basement."

"Please don't make me gag you." When I didn't respond, he said, "Thank you."

"You're literally the worst kidnapper ever if you feel the need to say please and thank you."

"Gag," he spat as he reached for the console.

Knowing I would be silenced in an unpleasant way, I slumped against the window. I would wait until he stopped, and I got an opportunity to escape.

Not long later, and past the suburbs, we entered through a tall, mechanical gate with pike-tips. Continuing along a concrete drive through a green lawn and perfectly placed trees, we finally stopped in front of a white, Victorian style, three-story home.

"We're home." Softness returned to his voice.

"This isn't my home."

"Yes, it is." He got out, then circled around to my side of the car and opened the door. I didn't move, nor did I look at him. He leaned down and wiped his thumb over my cheek. "You'll enjoy it here."

"Why? Because there's a yard to play in?"

He gripped my upper arm and pulled me out. "It's a better life."

I wiggled my wrists in the restraints as he forced me to the door. "Being your fuck slave isn't a better life."

As he punched a code into a keypad, he said, "I've asked you to be polite."

He led me into a spacious, neatly decorated foyer. From inside, the place looked larger than expected, and it felt more like a mansion. There was even a small, sparkling chandelier above, and pearly marble flooring below. The dark furniture was adorned with red velvet. A perfect place for a wealthy CEO to own a slave.

A warm smile returned to his features as he took my bound hands in his.

I immediately pulled free of his grasp.

The already tall man straightened. "I can see it may take a while before I can trust you to roam freely." Despite his height and strong build, he couldn't dominate me as Noah had. He couldn't even look at me in a way that would evoke fear.

"Do you need to train me properly, so I don't piss on the marble?"

He sighed and faced me, meticulously untying the rope. "I know you are under stress right now, but you are expected to behave in a pleasant manner."

"You're in-fucking-sane." I rubbed my hands, seeing the red where the bindings had been.

Jonah took the opportunity to pull me to his firm chest and kissed me. I pushed against him, but his arm had snaked around my lower back and locked me in place. The moment his hold loosened, I slapped him. The sound echoed.

He raised his hand to his cheek, narrowed eyes burning into me before they shifted further in the home.

Noah came into view on the beige, carpeted stairs. The black silk pajama pants he wore hung low, drawing attention to his defined abs. But the bounce to every slow step felt predatory. Even from afar, dominance rose from him like an invisible mist.

Jonah lowered his hand from his cheek. "Lizzie has accepted the opportunity." The pet name infuriated me even more. Only my parents, and sometimes Colette, had ever called me that.

While I had plenty to say to the prick, there was no way I would talk back while in Noah's presence. He would convince Jonah to turn me into a plaything at their club.

Noah's brow rose, and his sideways smirk fell upon me. "I look forward to working with you, Elizabeth."

I cowered against Jonah, who responded by turning and planting a peck against my cheek. "Thank you, Lizzie." Whether he thanked me for clinging to him, or not fighting the affection, I wasn't certain.

Noah sauntered into the kitchen, followed by Jonah, who'd happily taken my hand in his.

His feather-light lips roved along my jaw. "I need to clean up. You must be hungry. Have some breakfast with Noah." As he turned, I reached for him.

Noah spoke loud. "I'll take excellent care of her, Brother."

I slowly crossed the cold flooring to a stool at the stainless-steel island that separated us.

Noah went to the fridge and took out a bottle of a green beverage. By the way every muscle flexed as he raised it to drink, the pearly marble floor could have consumed his form and he would look like a statue of a god. And the sadistic prick knew it. When he lowered the bottle to the counter, a green trace was still on his upper lip.

"Come here." He licked his lip.

I had to retain some of my dignity. "Fuck you," I muttered. I couldn't let fear consume me; he would win. Both brothers would win.

His fingertips lowered to tap the counter. He stared at me, and his lips curled into a smile. "I. Didn't. Ask." He snapped and pointed to the area in front of his feet.

Hesitantly, I obeyed. After I slowly rounded the corner and came to stand between him and the counter, he pointed to the floor.

"On your knees," he ordered.

Like an owned bitch, I dropped to my knees and cast my gaze to the floor.

He gripped my hair and pulled, not hard, but enough so I looked up. "I don't like your language." His voice raised. "Look at me...good."

I wanted to claw my eyes out as I was forced to look into his deep, blue gaze.

"I gave you an order to go home, *not* to be Jonah's live-in girlfriend." His grip on my hair released before his fingertips trailed to my jawline. "Our training doesn't start until I have you all to myself, and I don't want his cock anywhere near you." A tent formed in his silk pants. It should be drained by the number of times he came inside me. When I flinched away, he grabbed my chin.

I said nothing, but turned my head. No doubt he could sense my tremble. From my periphery, he pulled his cock from his pants.

"I knew you were the type that loved to be dominated since I saw you." He clasped my hair again and pushed his erection against my lips. "Now give me a reason to reward that pretty cunt of yours."

Enraged, yet sexually excited at the same time, I opened my mouth.

He moaned as he slid in. "I love this beautiful mouth." With every stroke, he went deeper into my throat. I expected he would get it over with fast, like my bastard ex, but Noah's movements were slow, as though he relished every prolonged second. "Use your hands."

I obeyed and learned quickly to do whatever elicited a moan from him. Only then would he speed his movements, his legs shivering as I jacked along his length and gripped his balls. For a moment, there was almost affection in his features as he watched me, followed by a stern furrow of his brow and too-deep thrusts.

Hot seed exploded into my throat. He moaned, slow and deep, then pulled from my mouth. "Say 'thank you, Master.'"

"Thank you," I muttered.

He reached down and swooped me up, then spun me, so I leaned against the counter. After yanking the bottom of my black dress up, a hard slap stung my ass. "Address me properly."

"We're not in the fucking sex club for weirdos with whips."

Another slap, lower. Heat filled me as my skin stung.

I shook my head, eyes squeezed shut. No. He wouldn't be called Master.

His flat hand roved over the angry flesh, and he leaned against me. "You like pain too much for this to be punishment." He let his fingers dip into the moisture between my legs.

I shuddered and turned my head to look over my shoulder at him with a cold glare.

His predatory gaze shifted to my face. "Once I start training you, though, that pretty little cunt will be red from the riding crop if you so much as think of stepping out of line."

A beep came from above. Noah lowered my dress over my rear and reached for his green drink before he strode from the room.

As I considered the oddness of his sudden departure, Jonah stepped into view. Wet, brown hair hung messy over his forehead and flipped at the top of his ears. The subtle coconut smell of his soap wafted my direction.

Jonah seemed crazy, but harmless. But after being in Noah's presence, I backed to the corner of the kitchen.

"You're not wearing black," I muttered, looking down at his pajama pants that were as crimson as the velvet upholstery on the dark furniture.

Halfway across the kitchen, he stopped and glanced down to his pants. "I suppose not. Red's a good color too." He leaned back against the island with the same delight as when we were at the bar. When he mentioned a job then, I would never have expected this to be the opportunity.

"I want to go home."

His shoulders straightened, and he crossed his arms over his bare chest. "You aren't going back."

Mirroring him, but by a head shorter, I stood straighter and crossed my arms. "If you let me go now, I won't tell the cops."

The dimpled grin he flashed was one I wanted to slap right off. Not that my slap had bothered him previously. "You have no car, a bank account that wouldn't pay next month's rent, and an abusive ex you will return to out of desperation."

Every bit of information about me shouldn't have been known, not by someone without power. Of course the brothers would have power. They probably paid the bonuses of any cop or prying investigator, given their business in the sex industry.

"You must have gotten bad information," I spat.

Unperturbed by my anger, he shrugged. "At any rate, a contract you signed included a clause that you would not claim misdeeds against anyone, so long as you were always given opportunity to stop the relationship."

"I'm ending it."

"I see no safety ring. Anything goes when you have a safe word and the confidence to take the device off."

I shook my head. The ring hadn't been removed so I could enjoy a kidnapping fetish. He knew this, but planned to exploit me.

He pushed himself from the counter and strolled my direction. Desperate for anything to defend myself, I searched the countertop and found a block with knives.

Taking a hopeful opportunity, I rushed toward the knife set. My hand was less than a foot away before Jonah was on me, his arms locking mine down at my sides. Given his softer demeanor, I hadn't expected his grip to be so impossibly strong. Still, I kicked and fought, getting one graze to his shin before he had me bent on the opposite counter.

"I'll make sure nothing dangerous is accessible if you plan to resort to violence."

"Violence. You brought me here to be your rape toy, and I'm the violent one?"

"I would never touch you without your consent."

I pushed against the counter he had me pinned to. "You're touching me without my consent right now."

His mouth was next to my ear. "Can't we go back to when you were in my office and you wanted a job?"

"I wanted to go home."

"This will be your home." His breath traveled down my neck. "I can give you everything you need." The way his mouth went to the fleshy area where my neck and shoulder joined sent a shudder through me.

"And if it includes a rough fetish, I'm willing to accommodate that, too."

I attempted a kick to his shin but missed.

"What she needs is a healthy dose of humiliation." A voice came from across the counter to my left. Noah sauntered into view, already in a midnight blue, collared shirt and a black suit vest. He ran a hand through his hair, smoothing it.

"Fuck you." I panted, immediately regretting my response to the worst of the two brothers.

"And a gag until she learns some respect." He tossed a ball gag onto the counter. "I'm out to work."

Jonah nodded to his brother, followed by a low hum of desire as he kissed my shoulder. "You just need a little time with me, Lizzie."

There was no way they would get what they hoped for out of me. I wouldn't be the twins' Stockholm Syndrome deluded lover with a pet name. But I also wouldn't instigate wrath or fetish sex. Noah already owned my obedient will when he had me alone.

. . . .

ONCE NOAH HAD LEFT, Jonah led me up the curving staircase to a hall with several doors on both sides. The trim of the doors and baseboards was decorated in gold, adding to the elegance of the place. At the farthest door at the end of the hall, he took me into his room. A beep sounded when the door opened.

"You can let go of my hand now." I stepped away from Jonah.

He shut and locked the door with a key that he slid into the pocket of his pajama pants. "I laid out some clothes for you." In the center of the room was a four-poster, king-sized bed at least as tall as a thigh, with a seat at the end of it that looked more like a step to get up. Red curtains swooped at the top and were tied to the posts. Beneath the mattress, long black sheeting touched the floor. A mirror spanned the wall to my left, and I watched his reflection as he strode to the oddly tall bed.

Laid out over the scarlet duvet was a short black dress and lacy underwear. "I've ordered more for you." He hopped onto the bed next to the clothing. "Even something pink."

Some gifts they would be. He didn't even know what I liked. "Shoes?" I asked.

He grinned down at my bare feet. "You'll earn them soon enough."

"Where's my dog bed?" I continued to look around the immaculate room.

"Lizzie," his tone sounded more along the lines of a plea. "It's better this way. You'll be sleeping with me so long as you're good."

What an absolutely sick fuck. I'd make sure to suffocate him in his sleep if that was the case. "Is Noah coming back tonight?" I asked.

"No. Probably not until tomorrow noon."

Without Noah's predatory presence, I would get my chance to escape, given how obsessed Jonah was with me.

"Does that balcony door open?"

He grinned and got off the bed, immediately going to glass doors that overlooked decorative trees and a lawn. This was the back of the Victorian house, so I didn't know the layout, and the tall, piked fence wasn't within view.

With the same key as before, Jonah unlocked the double-doors and opened one. We were only on the second floor, although it felt like a high second floor, but I could come up with a way to climb down. Even without shoes, the well-kept lawn would be easy to run across, and there weren't lights that would expose me. At least, not that I saw.

Goose pimples formed on my skin, though the air was only slightly cold, probably in the sixties. It wouldn't get much colder at night. I went to lean against the balustrade, which ran along the large balcony that curved with the home. After a brief inspection of the lower level to either direction, I found mostly lawn that disappeared into a grey-cast due to mist. Even the pool below had a darker cast to it, but it was the largest private pool I'd ever seen.

The warmth of a hand roved my arm. From reflex, I jolted, though there was nowhere to go aside from closer to the balustrade. "It's chilly out here." Jonah slid a long-sleeved silk robe up my arms. Though it was short, at least my arms were covered from the damp chill. Already, I could feel a firm bulge against my lower back.

"Once the view is better, you'll see everything you get to enjoy." He swept the hair from my neck and kissed it.

He expected me to have sex with him. I knew that much. That would help with receiving his trust. I couldn't underestimate Noah's warning of harsh retribution to me if I did fuck Jonah, though. "I haven't been able to take my birth control," I lied. I'd made sure to have an IUD, so I didn't get pregnant with Marshal. Maybe that excuse would work in my favor.

"I don't mind." He continued, letting his mouth wander my shoulder. So, he thought I was some bitch to breed? Beyond crazy! He was beyond the crazy I'd believed him to be. He leaned closer to me.

"I'm not clean."

He inhaled. "You smell good to me." Despite my resentment, the feel of his hand as it wandered into the robe and into the neckline of the low-cut dress had a tingle rush between my legs. "You feel good too."

"I want a bath." I pushed his grip from my breast. I needed time to figure out what to do. I'd gone from bad sex with Marshal, to great—though humiliating—sex with Noah, who had planned to kidnap me, and now the other man who *did* kidnap me had the expectation of sex.

For reasons I couldn't count on both hands, this was horribly wrong. Noah had given me more orgasms in a few hours than Marshal had given me in months. He'd also forced them upon me through a manipulative trick he claimed to be perfectly legal. He or Jonah could legally fuck me no matter what I did to attempt to stop it. Hopefully Jonah wouldn't try to.

His hand firmly clung to my body, then lowered to the cloth of my underwear.

I squirmed. Jonah didn't need to feel any more of me than that. "I said a bath." I turned to glare at him.

He groaned his disappointment against my neck. "With or without bubbles?"

"With—and without you."

"Whatever you desire."

We returned inside where he proceeded to lock access to the balcony and went through a set of French doors into a large room with a bath the size of a jacuzzi set into the floor. It would be nice to live in a place like this, aside from the men I would be living with or the expectations of me being a whore.

He ran me a bubble bath and, despite it being large enough for both of us, he left me to the privacy I requested. I relaxed my head on a pillow as I pondered what to do. There was no way I could leave under the current conditions outside, though if Noah was gone often, I could likely figure out a way to escape Jonah. But with the distance to the nearest house I'd seen, I would need shoes.

Once I spent as much time as possible in the bath and rid myself of any possible residue of Noah, I took extra-long to dry my hair and got dressed in the new clothing Jonah had given me. It took all my calm to return to his room without a rude comment.

The handsome man was still in nothing more than his soft, red pants and sprawled on the bed, expectant. Already, the room had darkened from the curtains he'd pulled over the windows. In place of that light was the illumination of candles, which fragranced the room with vanilla.

So fucking mental!

In his hand was a small glass with ice and an amber beverage. At least he was getting drunk, though the glass seemed full. He placed it on the bedside table, where a fluke of a bubbly drink waited.

If romance was what he'd hoped to accomplish, it hadn't worked. No one had ever romanced me, and this was nothing more than a ruse. But what choice did I have but to go along with it?

With uncertainty in my own ability to deceive a man through flirtation, I went to Jonah and stepped up the seat to the large bed. I knew how to act to keep a man from going into a rage—well, mostly.

But the difference between my ex and Jonah was that I had wanted to please Marshal. Even if my agreeableness was to ensure our time together was tolerable, given Marshal's snappy responses.

Just as I collected myself to show interest, I glanced to the bedside table where a slender, dark vibrator lay behind a lit candle. Even after all the mental buildup to act interested in his endeavors, I scowled and said, "I hope you cleaned your last slave's fluids off that."

He groaned and raised both hands to rub his eyes. "I've never had a slave."

"What am I?"

He sighed before sitting up against the headboard and tugging me toward him. "Difficult." He pulled me to straddle his lap. "And unbelievably perfect." His fingertip traced the one-inch scar over my cheekbone. "You're safe here."

Shame caused me to turn from the touch. Mostly the shame of the night Marshal had lost control and hit me, but also the shame of a momentary satisfaction in the security Jonah offered. Under normal conditions, no man of his standing would want someone like me.

I swallowed, placing a hand to his shoulder to brace myself. Something inside wouldn't let me lie or seduce him. "You're nice, Jonah. I don't deserve you." In a way, it felt true—if he weren't a kidnapper.

"Raven wouldn't have sent you to me if that were true."

"Raven and I are acquaintances, at best." The reminder agitated me, and I moved off him to face away. "I'm sure you have plenty of opportunities with women."

"Not any opportunities that I would ever accept." His responses were always so casual, so easily straightforward.

"I'm sure plenty of women would love to be locked in your home and have a baby with you."

"Probably." He was behind me again. Lips to my shoulder. "But I want you." No argument would work with him. There would be no way of getting him to see things couldn't work as he had in mind.

"I signed a forty-day contract with Noah, then I'm free to go."

He nodded, grin stretching. "A contract I will take over since you were originally referred to me. After you've spent those days with me, we can go from there."

That was the problem. Noah had already made clear he would have that contract fulfilled, and it would begin when he had me to himself. This time in his home didn't count as time toward the agreement. The thought made me shudder. Noah or Jonah. What if there would be no escape and they could play games back and forth, claiming I could use a ring I'd gotten rid of at any point?

"I'm tired." Hopefully that would win the argument and give me time to think.

He rustled around behind me, pulling the covers to get under them. "Get in."

Most of the night I'd been awake, yet Jonah slept peacefully. At least I had gotten him to keep his distance with a pillow between us. At some point, I did succumb to exhaustion.

When I awoke, I rolled onto my side and searched for signs of Jonah. Nowhere.

The view out of the curtains had cleared to a blue sky and a vast, green yard. I still wore the short dress, and after a search, I found nothing else to wear aside from a long, plush robe hanging in the bathroom.

After I put it on and tied the sash tight, I tested the balcony door. Locked. With no other choice, I snuck to the door, listening for any noise in the hall.

Silence. But that ended the moment I opened the door, and a loud beep gave away my activity. Had they played this game with someone before? There didn't seem to be any other reason for the loud security. After a brief wait outside the door, I padded past one closed door on my left, then continued to the open area before the stairs. Again, I waited, peeking down to the room below. No movement, no sound.

Every creeping step felt as though I walked through land mines. At the lower level, I poked my head around the corner to the open dining room and kitchen. No one. This may have reeked of a trap, but Noah wasn't expected until later, and he was the one with the malicious cruelty to set up traps. I didn't hesitate to rush on the balls of my feet to the front door.

When I twisted the large handle, it opened without a beep. I continued forward, next to the white outer wall. Jonah's car—engine running and driver's side door open—was parked at the circle drive in front. Even if he came out and saw me, I'd have a head start. At that thought, I bolted to the open door and dove in.

I searched for the gearshift to put it in drive, first beside the wheel, then at my side. I bit my lip at the sight of the shifter. I didn't know how to drive a manual, but how hard could it be? When I hit the gas, it revved without moving, content to torment me with the fading hope of freedom.

I opened the door and got out, spotting a man in my periphery on the left. As I stayed locked in panic, he closed in. But I did nothing, even when he was right behind me. I released the door before a slow turn to see which twin waited behind me. I couldn't tell. They looked the same, especially when all my attention went to the shirtless torso.

"Left alone for a few minutes and you try to steal a car." The way his gaze roved over me in the robe was unnerving—like I was a piece of cake to be devoured. *Noah.*

"I wasn't stealing a car."

He let out a humored huff. "No, you were just attempting to take it for a joy ride." He pulled me by the sash, causing my face to land against his muscular chest and my stomach against the swell in his pants. "Feel how hard I am already? That's because I get to punish you."

I swallowed. "Jonah won't allow you to do that."

"Jonah's out buying you pretty things that I can bend you over and fuck you in." He tipped my chin, so I looked up to him. Smiling as the words sunk in. "Remove my belt." Had he put on suit pants just for this? It had been a cruel trick.

My hands shook as I gripped the buckle. The defiant part of me had to yank the end, so it tightened first. The added effort failed to get a response from him. An unwanted ache grew between my legs as my traitorous body responded to every perfect inch of his physique.

He held out his hand. Once I'd given the belt to him, he ordered, "Take off that robe."

"It's cold."

"I'll warm you."

I blushed, but obeyed, letting it fall to the ground. My chest swelled with every nervous breath. I hated myself for craving his touch. Already my skin prickled from the cool air.

His gaze never left mine. "Take off your clothes." When I hesitated, his eyes narrowed. The warning was enough that I worked the stretchy dress down my body, leaving only the matching black lace underwear.

"If I have to remove anything, I'll have you bound by that pretty jewelry again."

I reached behind to unsnap the bra. Still, his stare forced mine as the skimpy fabric fell. Then I worked the underwear down my legs.

"Bend over the hood."

I glanced down to the belt. He couldn't be serious. There was no way I'd let him belt me like a misbehaved child. I covered my chest with my arm.

One side of his mouth flicked upward. "Every time you refuse an order or cover yourself, I will add an extra day to the forty I *will* have with you. And I'll use this belt on your ass until it's flaming red every one of those days."

"Jonah already said you aren't getting your forty days." I would accept Jonah if it guaranteed safety from whatever Noah planned.

"He's wrong. Now turn around unless you want even more punishment."

Lip quivering, I turned, bent forward, and placed my palms on the warm hood of the car.

"Wasn't that nice of me to warm it for you?" He pulled my hips outward. "Spread your legs more."

I obeyed, squinting when he gave no other order.

The first swat stung and caused me to jolt forward. Then came the second, lower and harder. Then the third that landed at my slit, causing my first wince of pain. But I couldn't lie to myself and deny how good it felt, and he seemed to know that. Another landed in the sensitive region.

"You like that, don't you, slave?"

My long hair curtained forward as I shook my head. He wouldn't get the satisfaction of knowing I enjoyed it.

The belt fell near my foot. His black shoes came close between my heels. I heard his zipper lower. "If you're lying to me, I'm not going to let you cum." With one hand on my hip, his other guided my back downward until my cheek and breasts were to the warm metal. His length slid along the juices he'd caused. His responding words were spoken with slow certainty. "You lied to me."

I panted as he teased my entrance with his cock. As though he knew it was tormenting, he kept the movements slow, grazing over the nub that ached for more friction. With his fingers digging into my hips, he began to rock into me, pushing me forward on Jonah's car.

"I can't wait to have you to myself, so I can use this cunt until you can't sit." He pulled back then slammed his length all the way into me.

I whimpered from the sting where he'd belted me. I half-wondered if all his threats to take me to a training session where he could mercilessly abuse me were a lie. Of all the times in my life I had been fucked, they never felt as good as Noah's mix of bliss within me. What felt good sky-rocketed in intensity when he flipped me onto my back and pushed me further onto the hood and slowly rocked into me—each time built up the certainty of my release as his steady pumps hit my g-spot.

As my need built higher, and release drew near, he went deep, pulsing seed into me. "Liars don't get gratification." His smile made me wish I could punch him.

"You fucking prick."

"You have no idea how much of a fucking prick I can be." He rose from atop me and pulled his pants up. "Put these back on." He tossed my bra and panties at me.

They were better than being naked and seething. After moving from the car, I turned and put them on. The band around my neck tugged, but before I had time to react, he had it off me. At least he was kind enough to remove it and the bracelets. My satisfaction ended when something wider and softer encircled my neck.

A fucking collar?

"I think this one will do nicely for now. Come with me."

I yanked at the thick leather, trying to get it off, but it too seemed to have a lock that prevented removal. Before I could shriek my frustration, a pull to it had me struggling against the leash.

"I'll have you on hands and knees if you don't follow willingly."

At that threat, I followed behind him as we rounded the large Victorian home. At least this gave me an opportunity to better study the layout. It looked like what must have been a mansion a century ago, but it must have been built only a few years ago. Tall, sculpted pillars, thick enough to hold during escape, stretched up to the second floor. A small building the size of a garage to one side, and further inward, the massive pool that could be seen from Jonah's balcony. It could possibly be jumped down to if the weather were warmer.

Noah sat on a wide, leather cushioned lounger. "Come here." As his fist turned to reel in the leather leash, I obeyed. Every step filled me with more resentment at how he continued to humiliate me. My effort to hug my mostly exposed body provided no covering or heat.

"Hands behind your back," he snapped. "Unless you want me to give you the matching wrist cuffs early."

I tucked my hands behind my back.

There would be no hiding from his lustful leer. "Soon enough, your wrists and ankles will be cuffed to the posts of my bed. And if you're good..." He reached out to stroke my lower leg. "I might let you cum after I've thoroughly used you."

"Get your forty days over with, then."

"I'm enjoying this too much." He moved to the side of the lounger. With a smirk, he patted the spot beside him. "Jonah won't be home for a while. Join me unless you're planning to go for a swim."

I wasn't a glutton for punishment either way, but I'd rather be warm than shivering from a cold pool. I slumped onto the chair, facing outward to the expanse of grass. If it weren't for his threats of what he had in store, Noah wasn't all that bad. He must have known I had that thought by the way he jerked me down, yanked my panties to the side, and fucked me again, whispering sweet promises of torment with every thrust.

Once he'd had his fill, teased me, and left me unfulfilled, he led me to a downstairs shower, watching to make sure I didn't touch myself. If that weren't humiliating enough, he made me sit on the counter in the kitchen, wearing only the robe of Jonah's—open in the front—with ice he would periodically stroke over me as he made breakfast, though the hour was a bit late for the meal given it was already afternoon.

"This wouldn't be a problem if you had been honest with me." He placed the food in covered serving dishes, then lowered to his knees in front of me, running his mouth up my inner thigh after he'd removed the locked anklets.

"You're a sadist," I whispered as he heated my slit with warm breath.

"Just wait until I show you how much of a sadist I am." His eyes seemed to dance with joy as his tongue slid over my flesh. But he only took me to another edge of gratification, sensing the moment I quivered before he stood.

When his phone buzzed, he ordered me to put my underwear and dress on. Once I'd put my clothes on, Noah pulled me close for a kiss, impassioned yet brief.

A door beeped, possibly a garage entry.

"Don't even think about fucking him," Noah growled as he turned.

In a way, I wanted to see what Noah would do if I did fuck Jonah. Was it jealousy or simply his need for control? Either way, I had no doubt his warnings of what he planned to do to me once I was at his mercy were very, very real. But real enough not to test him?

As I placed my plate of food on the table, steps came from behind. They were soft, and I'd begun to sense the difference between Noah and Jonah's gaits. Noah continued past, wearing a collared shirt unbuttoned at the top. He dropped his plate at the spot in front of mine, buttoning a sleeve cuff once he'd sat.

"Lizzie." Jonah's hand grazed my lower back. The bangs of his hair tickled my temple as he pecked my cheek.

I stiffened; my gaze locked ahead on Noah. Whatever expression he had was unreadable. Why would he even think Jonah wouldn't try to sleep with me? Telling Jonah about my encounters with Noah would risk me ending up in the dungeon before my four months were complete. I knew better than to do that.

"I got you a present," Jonah said, placing a box on the table next to my plate. Before I had a chance to open the large, flat box, Jonah had already stridden from the room.

Noah lifted his fork, tip pointed to the box. "Open it."

I removed the lid. Under a layer of tissue paper was a pale, pink dress—a stretchy, thin, lacy texture that was far too short.

"Told you it was something I'd be fucking you in," Noah said low, before dipping his fork into eggs. His eyes narrowed. "Put it on for me."

I chewed my lower lip for a moment, but clutched the dress and went to the bathroom. After donning the expensive silken fabric, I took my time to examine myself. A rich man's prize stared back from the mirror. By the length and the sheerness that showed my black underwear, I had to assume it was not suited for public wear. As I stepped out, I almost bumped into Jonah, who carried several tall bags from a designer store.

He stopped and flashed me a hungry glance. "You look beautiful."

"Thanks for the lingerie." I stepped past him.

As if he didn't catch the sarcasm, he said, "You're welcome, Lizzie." He continued toward the stairs with his bags.

"Sit down and eat," Noah ordered from the table.

I returned and sat, pretending to ignore his stare as I sliced my fork into a pancake. Only the sound of scraping forks and Jonah's steps interrupted our meal. How much had Jonah purchased for five trips up and down the stairs? And I doubted I wanted to know what all he had chosen for me to wear as his live-in whore.

Noah's dominant stare made me regret glancing toward him as he stood and carried his dishes. When he reached my side of the table, his hip rested on it. "Enjoy wearing clothes while it lasts. You won't get any once you're training with me."

Against all reason, my stomach dipped. Why his words excited me seemed bizarre. But I knew it wouldn't be a romantic getaway where I got the privilege to be nude. It would be another one of his torments. The dress had been a kindness from Jonah. Maybe I should have been thankful I was permitted to wear anything at all.

Once the kitchen was silent, I took my dishes to the sink and washed them before moving onto the pots, and finally the counters. A glorified maid with the luxury of wearing lingerie. I'd seen job postings for such a position, and it seemed that was what I would be good for.

When I turned, one of the twins leaning against the kitchen entry startled me. A dimpled grin stretched across his face. *Jonah*. In a way, that charming smile made him twice as handsome as Noah. With hands in his pant pockets, he slowly strolled over.

"I didn't think that was an exceptional dress until I saw you in it."

"Thanks." I looked down and attempted to flee the kitchen.

He blocked my departure, pinning me to the same area where Noah had tormented me.

My heart raced at the thought of what Jonah expected as he pressed against me. His hungry gaze suggested more than a simple compliment about the dress I wore. As though I weighed less than a feather, he gripped my waist and lifted me onto the counter.

"We shouldn't." I turned my cheek to his lips as he attempted to kiss me.

His soft grip on my jaw pulled my face to his again. "Why not?"

"Noah," I whispered.

"So what if he sees?" His hard dick already pressed against my thigh. "He gets off on that sort of thing. Just like I get off on being watched."

"I don't." I turned away from him again.

"I'll be quick about it."

I squirmed back, pushing him away. "Stop!"

To my shock, he backed away. "As you wish." With a sheepish smile, he said, "Come upstairs so you can see what I got you."

· · · ·

ONCE WE'D ENTERED JONAH'S room, he looked to the large mirror to my reflection as he removed his tie and placed it in his wide, dark dresser. I'd never known a tie to be so appealing, or for one to look so good as it slid off a man. A game of seduction. That was all this was. One of his and Noah's individual games to have and toy with me.

But winning over Jonah was the ticket to my leaving, something I had to remember. I thought back to all the times Raven had brought her lovers to Colette's, how much they adored her. I could do that, right? But Raven acted more dominant like Noah. It would be easier to play a part with someone like him. Jonah didn't make demands. To be with him was like figuring things out for myself, not knowing a particular direction to go.

"Noah helped you remove those silver bands." He went to his bedside table and bent down to open the doors to reveal a tiny refrigerator and bar items.

I gripped my left wrist. "He did."

Jonah pulled out a wine glass and filled it with a bubbly drink, then a frosty small cup that he filled with what I assumed to be the same bourbon he had the night before. "You're even more beautiful without the adornment." He unbuttoned the cuffs of his sleeves as he faced me.

"Thank you." I blushed at the way his gaze continued to rove over my minimally dressed form.

He grinned as he handed me the glass of champagne. "I filled the bath for you."

I took a sip of the cool, tangy beverage and glanced at the bathroom. There was more than a small flutter in my chest as I went that direction, most likely from the champagne. There wasn't a lock to the doors, but I closed them all the same. He hadn't bothered me last night, so I doubted he would now.

A mound of bubbles looked as though it grew from the floor from the large tub. After dipping into the swell of suds, I sought the coconut scented bar of soap at the edge. I imagined this must be the way women who lived in luxury spent half their day, fancy drinks at the ready, lounging in baths, and—

The door clicked open from behind me.

—and getting fucked by whoever afforded them such accommodations. There would always be a catch to receiving anything. With a low sigh, I took another drink. *Remember, he is the ticket out of here.*

Bubbles swayed as Jonah dipped behind me.

Gathering my strength to smile, I turned to see him, champagne bottle in one hand, his own drink in the other. Whether his dick was at attention, I would have to wait and find out.

"I hope I gave you enough time to relax." He poured more champagne into my glass. He hadn't, but I'd noticed he was a more eager man after a drink. Though I'd not yet seen him drunk, which I found interesting.

"Of course." I took a long gulp, releasing a small smile.

Then he came close, arms wide to either side of me as he emptied his hands. "Good." Too quickly, his mouth captured mine, swirling in the flavor of bourbon.

I blindly made several attempts to set the champagne fluke on the edge so it didn't fall. The moment the kiss broke, I sucked in a breath of air.

"The thought of coming home to you has had me riled all day." Firm hands already pushed my legs apart and kneaded my thighs. "And, oh, the things I chose for you to wear."

Pretending to enjoy his touch wasn't too difficult, not as my need came blasting back to me. Refusing him would be damn near impossible—something I could easily blame the champagne for.

"What did you get?" I asked, not fighting as his hard manhood drew near to my entrance. Even my back arched in response to the way his mouth grazed below my jaw.

"A little of everything."

"Then shouldn't we—" *wait?*

I couldn't finish before he'd plunged into me. There was the answer, and my misdeed that Noah would punish me for. But I wanted this, and the only person to blame was Noah for the toying with my desperation he'd caused me for hours. What was the worst he could do? Punish me more with desperation?

"God, Lizzie..." Jonah pumped deep, pushing me up onto the cushioned edge, wiping the sudsy bubbles from my chest so he could find a nipple to take into his mouth.

Faking an interest hadn't ever received its opportunity. Now I lay back, my hands clawing for purchase on the soft carpeting mat beneath my head. Legs coiled around his hips as bubbles bobbed forward with his thrusts. Noah could toy with my desperation all he wanted, but he couldn't worship my body the way Jonah could.

To hide my shame of gratification, I bit into the back of my hand, only to add a painful sensation that further fueled my cravings for release. Within three minutes, Jonah had me moaning against my hand in pleasure, squeezing my walls around his thick girth—milking explosions of cum as he slammed deep.

His hum tickled my chest. "You felt so good that I couldn't slow it down."

I had to blame the champagne for the sex happening at all. But a bliss bubbled into me as I accepted the next worshiping kiss.

It wasn't until we were in his bed again that I noticed the mirror above—one he took full advantage of watching as he had me again. This time, I couldn't blame the champagne for how much I wanted the pleasure he provided.

Upon waking, my resolve to reject Jonah and to escape returned. Though, it was a struggle once he found his spot on top of me, once again bringing my toes to curl in a way I hadn't fathomed possible. After he'd thoroughly pleasured us both, he collapsed beside me on the bed and tucked me into the crook of his shoulder.

After we laid there a while, he stretched and sat up. "I got you something."

"Thanks." I found myself curious of what he'd gotten, but also a little agitated at his expectation for me to wear lingerie and fuck him. I couldn't deny that I would do it gladly under other circumstances, though.

"You don't even know what it is." He stood. "Follow me."

I bundled the red satin sheet around me as I followed him to the corner. A door within the wall slid open.

"Go in." He stepped out of my way.

I walked into the room that lit overhead. It took a moment for my eyes to adjust to the closet the size of a small room. A small section of shoes and boots—all high heels and varying in color and design. I went to the area where short dresses hung. They were all soft fabrics I would only have ever dreamt of being able to afford. When I turned, he was looking into a wide drawer with neatly placed garters. Numerous other drawers lined the wall.

He grinned; one cheek revealed a small dimple. "Garters, underwear sets, lingerie—" he walked further in and opened another drawer. "Stockings."

I began to realize he chose items for me as he went. He pressed a button on the bare back wall, and it slid open. He stepped in, and the overhead light turned on. An entire corner had an angled mirror to give multiple views of oneself.

"Makeup is here." He pulled a cabinet from the wall and pushed it in front of the mirrors. Then he opened a cabinet to pull out a chair and set it in front. "I would love it if you put these on and wore makeup for me."

He placed several items on the desk before a slow step my direction.

I forced a swallow and turned my attention to the black and pink items he'd laid out for me to wear. I hadn't expected the kiss he placed on my cheek, nor the next, or the next, before his mouth was to mine.

"Please," he whispered against my lips. The want in his eyes flashed like Noah's. Why did the brothers have to be identical? A tinge of fear set in at the thought of Noah's discovery of my actions with Jonah. The thought that reminded me of my ticket out of here being Jonah's trust.

"Okay." I nodded.

"I'll give you privacy." He stepped out of the dressing room, and the door slid closed. The makeup was higher quality than I could ever have imagined having access to. A privilege. I'd wanted clothes. I hadn't expected anything so expensive or that they would be chosen for me. In some ways, he'd been charming, but now I felt like his little whore, prettied up like a doll. I held the items and slumped down on the chair.

First, I put on makeup, the whole time my mind reeled. As I stroked foundation over my face, I thought about why this life of luxury wasn't acceptable for me.

I continued, selecting the perfect brushes to add color to my eyes and cheeks. Finally, I applied a pink shade of lipstick. Not too bold. With a sigh, I ran my fingers over the lingerie. So smooth. I lowered the sheet to put on the outfit.

The black lingerie skirt with a pastel pink bow on the front was more of decoration and didn't cover but the top half of my backside. The pink push-up bra barely covered my nipples. No panties. Next was the garter, black with pink bows at the top seam in front and back. The silky, black stockings slipped on like butter, though they had a thong toe, so my toes were exposed. Hopefully, Jonah didn't have a foot fetish.

Something else was on the back edge of the desk. Pink and shimmering. At the same instant I picked it up, I threw it back down. He hadn't wanted me to wear underwear because he wanted me to have a pink jewel butt-plug. No—one-thousand times and more. Never! Nor would he stick any appendage of his in there. Not even to pretend to win his trust would I agree to that.

After I examined myself in the outfit he'd laid out—minus the butt-plug, I couldn't help but admire how good I looked. Marshal never bothered to comment when I wore make-up or wore lingerie, yet Jonah wanted it. Should I feel flattered?

On my way through the closet, I snatched a lacy thong from a drawer and slid it on. Jonah couldn't complain that it interrupted the view too much.

He was already waiting with a white box outside the closet door when I came out. A slight hitch caught his breath. "You're beautiful—I take it you didn't like the jewel I left for you?"

"No."

"I was hoping to see a little more." He grazed my skin until his finger hooked into the front of the thong.

"I need it shaved." After all, Noah had been the one to bind and shave me the last time.

Jonah gave me a quizzical look. "I'm certain we'll be able to take care of that." He extended the box to me.

I opened the gift and pulled the tissue from it. Inside was a black, soft leather cat mask that extended to a little below the cheekbone.

"Go on, there's more." He took the mask and turned it in his hand. Even as he stepped around behind me, I caught his reflection admiring the mask. It seemed he was a bit overly fond of it.

I moved more tissue to reveal a black leather collar with a pink bow which matched my attire. Attached to the center of the bow was a bell that jangled with the slight movement of lifting it. Had this been a simple outfit to wear in the bedroom, he would have given me one and it would have been used last night.

"I got you twenty, so they always match your clothing. You're going to look absolutely beautiful." He raised the mask to cover the top half of my face. The ears up top were small, but the eye holes were wide and shaped like cat-eye glasses. He placed the mask and secured it in a few spots on the back of my head. Once he stepped me closer to the wall mirror, he roved over my reflection with predatory eyes. With a soft touch, he guided my hair to one side. "The collar."

I raised it to his extended hand. The embarrassment of the sight made me realize how horrible this would be. I couldn't do this, not even as an act.

He put the collar around my neck, gently, so as not to tangle my hair. "You will need to tie your hair back while this is on."

"Will I always be wearing this?" I asked. My tone may have been out of place and hostile, but why should he receive obedience or respect from me?

"This is just for when we're on cam."

"Cam?" I spun to glare up at him. "Camera? You would expose me like that? This is how you aim to get your use out of a contract I signed?" I was too angry to do anything a well-behaved slave or cat would do.

"We'll be wearing masks. Besides, you're going to get comfortable practicing in role for a day or two first." He rubbed my cheek and stepped close. "We can start in short spans. Once you try it, you'll love it. Besides, no one will ever know who you are."

I attempted to take off the collar, but it had been locked in place. "Take it off."

"I think you need time to see that you will like it."

I reared back to slap him, but this time, he caught my hand.

With a soft grip on my wrist, he said, "This is all I ask of you. Please, for me." He released his hold, but there was no waver. He intended for me to dress like a pet for a camera and be exposed to whoever wanted to view me being fucked. Marshal's accusations of me being a slut would be proven true. No, I wouldn't let a single one of his insults be proven true.

When Jonah didn't allow me a dress to wear, I proceeded to don a satin robe. I said nothing to him, not through breakfast, which I chose to eat oatmeal instead of anything he offered to cook. He didn't even receive another glance from me, not for the entirety of the day.

I still wore the humiliating outfit, all aside from the mask that had no locking device to be kept on me. By late afternoon, after Jonah had given me a day to myself, he found me on the lounger wrapped in a warm blanket, staring across the pool.

He already wore his clothing, a suit vest over a silky blue collared shirt that matched his eyes. Handsome. He was disturbingly handsome. And the man had one fucked up fetish.

"I have to go to work soon but should be back before morning. Come inside and have dinner with me, please."

I got up to leave before he could pull me against him. He didn't let me go, though. It felt like those times Marshal would sometimes bully me from passing when I was too upset to remain in a room.

When Jonah's arm did coil around me, I pushed him straight toward the pool. I hadn't expected his hold would remain, and we both fell together. The crash into the cold water stung me like knives that lasted far too long, and I was embarrassed that he had to pull me out.

He rushed inside, returning with a few towels, one he immediately wrapped me in. By the time we made it indoors, me shivering and removing my robe, Jonah already had his vest off and shirt unbuttoned. I clung to the towel, teeth chattering. How could the water be that cold?

I rushed toward the stairs, blocked by Noah—wearing nothing but black boxers. "Where do you think you're going?"

My quaking worsened. "To Jonah's room."

"Oh, you'll be going to *your room*."

"Noah," Jonah called from the dining area. "Let her get dried off."

Noah's narrowed eyes focused on the collar at my neck as he swatted it with his fingers. "Your little pet needs some discipline, Jonah."

Jonah was in nothing more than a towel by the time he came to my side. "I'll stay with her tonight."

Noah huffed. "I'm not letting you stay home from work to coddle her."

I took a step backward, realizing Noah would be in charge of me.

"The expense of the ruined clothing is being docked from your future pay. And these collars are very expensive."

Jonah started, "It was—"

"An ill-behaved pet." Noah pulled my towel from my grip. "And if you aren't willing to train her properly, then I will."

I clutched my scantily clad body, attempting to hide behind my arm. Noah was the type of man I couldn't argue with. He was also the type of man I wouldn't dare push into a pool.

Jonah stepped between us. "I won't let you do that to her."

"I won't do anything she doesn't deserve." Noah let his gaze linger on me. "I'll simply take her to her room and let her out for breaks while you're gone."

"That room is for fun, not punishment."

I swallowed. What room was this that Noah spoke of?

"Then she's going under your bed for a while." Noah stepped out of the way. "Come on, pet." He went up the stairs.

When I looked at Jonah, he only sighed and motioned for me to follow Noah. I didn't move, though. Not an inch. Not until Jonah caressed my lower back. "It's better if you're in my room until I return."

With reluctance, I slowly followed Noah into Jonah's room. Upon arrival at their home, there had been a curiosity as to the height of Jonah's bed. That curiosity turned to horror once Noah began removing the black skirt sheet.

Vertical black bars, like those of a jail cell, stood like nightmarish pillars holding up the bed. Lost in my dread, the smooth fabric Jonah placed in my trembling hands fell straight to the floor.

"I'm not getting into that cage."

"No, you're not. That is for good pets." Metal creaked as Noah opened a door to what I'd thought was a seat at the end of the bed. It was connected to another cage section, but only the width of my body and only knee height, so about four inches shorter than the part beneath the bed.

"Jonah..." I turned to him, but he was in his closet.

"If he can't see to minimal training like this, then I'll take charge of you." Noah pointed to the cage. "And I will enjoy all forty days of it and the months that follow. Now, unless you want that too soon, put on the clothes he gave you and get in."

It seemed odd Jonah wouldn't mind me being naked in front of Noah, but I quickly changed from my wet lingerie into the pink silk camisole and matching boy shorts. A grip to the collar from behind had me thankful for Jonah's presence as he removed it. When I glanced at the wall mirror, he didn't return a look.

I swallowed as my attention returned to Noah, who tapped his bare foot next to the small cage.

Jonah kissed my cheek. "I'll be back before morning."

"You can't be serious, Jonah." I gripped his wrist.

"This will be fine. You'll enjoy it." Jonah's response would have infuriated me had Noah not been there. I could have argued, pleaded, gotten out of the humiliation, but with Noah there, Jonah didn't budge.

Noah leaned against the door. "I'll get the riding crop if you continue to disobey."

I went in front of Noah, lowered to my hands and knees, and crawled in.

After he closed the cage door, he said, "One more fuck-up from you and it's to my dungeon." The lights turned off when they left the room.

It felt like hours I lay on the cold plastic panel curled up in the cage meant for punishment. Everything with Jonah would have been fine had Noah not interrupted. He wouldn't let Jonah forgive and forget. *Training*, Noah claimed. What I'd foolishly signed a contract for. Forty days and three months for them to do any and everything to me, and with Noah, literally anything was possible.

Dim lighting piqued my interest as the bedroom door opened. The rapid gait was that of Noah, the arrogant prick's smirk plastered on his chiseled face. He wore only soft, dark pants.

"Oh, how I love this," he drawled. "You receiving baby steps into the training I'll give you soon enough, while Jonah slowly accepts it's the only way." He opened the door. "Get out, pet."

I crawled backward out of the cage. Once I stood in front of him, I refused to make eye contact.

"Be thankful I'm not ordering you to remain on hands and knees." The back of his hand brushed over where my hardened nipple poked the satin camisole. "We're going to have so much fun while he's gone." He swooped me close for a kiss I didn't fight. He gripped my still-damp hair. "My cock has been hard since the moment you pushed him into the pool. Follow me so I can bend you over and fuck that pretty little cunt."

I obeyed and followed him out and down the hall, slowing at the sight of where a seven-foot section of wall had disappeared to reveal bars like those of a prison cell.

Noah went to the end and pushed something that had the wall slide closed before I could see into the shadowed space. "You aren't supposed to see that yet."

"When am I supposed to see it?" My arms crossed in front of my breasts.

"When you're wearing a pretty little kitty outfit and I'm fucking you through the bars as you mewl for me."

Nausea filled me at the thought. "You lied to get me to sign that contract."

He shrugged. "You took off your ring. This was all in the fine print, and you were given plenty of warning that the removal of that ring wasn't a wise move. I even gave you a safe word. You can say it any time you want this to end." I recalled no such safe word. If he had, it must have been in code.

"I don't want to play your games anymore."

He crossed the hall to open his door. "That's what all slaves say." He winked. The playfulness was equally as disturbing as everything else he'd ever done. I continued in after him, halting when his grip landed on my wrist. Then he turned, my nose landing against his firm chest and savoring the sandalwood scent of his skin. Capturing me close, he secured soft cuffs over my wrists to the opposing elbows behind my back.

His firm manhood pressed against my lower stomach as he pulled me uncomfortably tight. "You've been a bad little slave."

I feared he spoke of discovering my sex with Jonah. Would Jonah have told him?

"I can do anything I want so long as there are no marks for Jonah to see." He ground against me. "Until I have you alone in my dungeon. Then you have no idea what's waiting for that pretty cunt." The tone of his voice brought a tingle straight down to my core, but to believe he wouldn't torment me once he had me alone would be foolish. "Let's go outside."

I cringed at the thought of how cold it might be at night, but I obeyed, walking to the balcony door and waiting as he opened it. An immediate chill hit me outside. It was a continuation from Jonah's balcony, but this opened to right above the pool lit from within. I glared down at the pool. Even if it were to be a last resort, that might be my only means of escape if I had to go through with their plans for me.

"You don't know how hard it was to watch you down there. Knowing I had to wait on Jonah to leave so I could have you."

"Watching me like a stalker?"

The prod of his cock against my backside moved me forward to the balustrade. I couldn't even catch myself if I fell over into the icy pool.

"I didn't give you permission to speak." He slid my shorts down my legs, tapping my leg so I lifted one, then the other, before he kicked the bottoms to the side. "Spread your legs."

I obeyed. Soft cuffs secured my ankles to the cold posts. For too long, he left me there shivering in nothing more than a loose camisole, but all too soon, his steps returned.

"This will be so much more fun once you're in my pillory."

His pillory? Before I had time to look over my shoulder in horror, pain from a lash of his crop stung my backside.

I shrieked, more from surprise than pain.

"Count and thank me, slave."

"No," I spat.

Another sting. "You're getting ten, and they don't start until you start counting and thanking me."

Another swat, more painful and right on my slit before I cried, "One, thank you."

"Address me properly."

To my humiliation, I said what he wanted. "Thank you, Master." And he swatted me ten more times.

"Such an obedient little slave *sometimes*." The warmth of his hands as they dipped under my top to cup my breasts was a welcome sensation. His cock rubbed against the still stinging flesh. "I knew you would love that," he purred. He entered me and pushed my body, so it hung forward.

Despite how cold I should have felt, or how angry I should have been, all I could feel was the bliss of how he pistoned into me. I had to use all my abdominal effort not to hunch forward during the pounding. Vibration accompanied the hand that gripped my mound.

"I'm considering letting you cum for how you tossed Jonah into the pool." His words filled me with excitement. He'd tormented me for so long the day before, to give me an orgasm, and with all the sensation flowing through me—

Left hand splayed, he lifted me by my sternum, connecting my back to his chest. With a jerk forward, he found his release. Nipping at my shoulder, he whispered, "We have a while for you to earn yours."

Noah didn't lie. He spent the night toying with me as he rested and cooked and even took a bath with me. When he finally did let me cum, he made sure I wouldn't forget it as all that pent up need came roaring from within me, over and over again. After he'd thoroughly tormented and filled me with unimaginable ecstasy, he returned me to Jonah's room.

"I can't wait to see you playing Kitty tomorrow." The kiss he pulled me into wasn't one of goodbye. It was deep and passionate, the sort of kiss that only happened in movies. The sort that could make a woman crave more. But he simply ordered me back into my punishment cage less than an hour before Jonah returned home.

The darkness in Jonah's eyes when he stepped in and saw me was worrisome. I didn't know if it was anger or an uncontrollable need to mount and fuck me. Before he came to me, he rushed into the closet, clattering around before he rushed out, a bit disheveled. The moment I backed out of the cage, he swooped me upright for a passionate embrace.

"I need to shower. Put on the Kitty outfit I set out. Red lipstick and thick, lining on your eyes, low ponytail. And get in the larger cage." For once, it was a dominant order and too strange for his usual demeanor. It felt almost as though Noah had come in to trick me, but I'd caught onto the subtleties of their differences.

As Jonah demanded, I put on make-up and the outfit—minus the sapphire blue butt-plug. The lingerie pieces he'd set out were a deep blue and white. Bows on the garter, lingerie skirt that ruffled and only reached halfway down my rear, and a cup-less bra. This was even more whorish than the last time.

I didn't get in the cage, though. I'd had enough of that, and there was only so much humiliation I would allow him to subject me to. When he stepped out of the bathroom, he'd put on a different suit vest—a dark blue silk one with small etchings on it, along with a matching tie and black suit pants.

It was a breathtaking look on him, especially the way his wet hair fell forward, almost to his brow.

"I told you I wanted you in the cage, Kitty." He took a moment to guzzle in the sight of me, causing a blush despite my anger. With more urgency than I'd ever seen in him, he strode toward where I stood near his bed.

"I won't." I held my ground on the issue, unyielding even when his body was to mine, and his hand squeezed my backside, creeping inward to my rear hole.

"You aren't wearing the plug."

"I won't do that either."

His tone softened. "We can start out slow."

Or not at all where those things are involved.

He went to his bedside table and took out a navy-blue collar with a bell-adorned bow and the black cat mask. No mind was paid to my responding scowl as he placed the collar on my neck. Once the mask was on, he didn't have to see my annoyance, anyway.

"Oh, Kitty, you are such a little cum-slut."

I wanted to slap him, not for the painful pinch to my nipples he proceeded to squeeze, but for the insult. But the thing that raced through my mind before slapping him was Noah's pillory. I wouldn't risk that.

"Say it, say you're my little slut."

With a head shake, I said, "I'm no one's slut."

"Alright."

Sometimes, his willingness to accept my defiance struck me as odd. Wasn't he supposed to demand certain behaviors from me? Force me?

With a sigh, his thumbs circled my aching nipples. "Maybe next time?" When I didn't respond, he pointed to a spot near him on the bed and ordered, "On your back, head over the edge here."

At least that wasn't too embarrassing. My obedience brought a smile to his handsome features. When he towered above my head, the bulge of his erection brushed against my cheek.

His splayed hands were already gliding over the contours of my chest and stomach. He stepped back and lowered so his lips met mine. The kiss was rushed, and he speedily continued toward my breasts, not placing his weight on me, but sliding his coconut scented chest to touch my face. He took my breasts into his strong hands as he sucked a nipple, twirling his tongue on the left one as he traced his thumb over the pebbled tip of the other. My responding moan and the arch of my back had him squeezing and sucking harder, adding a hint of teeth.

After worshiping my breasts, he continued further, his firm hands gripping my sides as they slid past my waist. God, it felt so good when he grabbed my thighs and pulled them upward as his warm tongue met my nub and trailed the length of my folds. Even more as he lapped and sucked with earnest, bringing a moan to my lips.

With his groin hovering over my face, his breath tickled my sensitive skin as he said, "Pull my cock out."

Without hesitation, I went to work on his pants tightened by his firm manhood. It was out and velvety soft against my cheek within seconds. He pulled me more towards the edge as he stroked it over my lips, gently pushing them apart to take him in. The bell on my collar tinkled as he began a slow rhythm in and out.

His attention returned to my slit, maneuvering his tongue in ways I loved. Something about the abundance of sensations sent me on the edge of gratification and had my hips rocking against his face. Right now, this was heaven, and he was a sex god. My moan melted against his cock as every one of my muscles tightened. The orgasm unleashed had come so powerfully, I continued to shudder long after he stood upright and slowly continued in my mouth, deeper so I nearly gagged until he held my head to angle just right to take him further.

"I love watching my cock in your throat, little slut." With those words, his eyes darkened, and he thrust deeper and faster, causing the jingle to speed up before it was a constant sound. I could barely breathe, and any effort to squirm away was met with a harsh twist to the peak of a nipple. Every several thrusts he pulled back enough to give me a desperate breath before he began to pound some more, somehow having avoided my gag reflex by the way he held my head as he fucked my mouth.

This was his slutty Kitty fetish? He thought I would be enduring this? I felt like I was close to passing out when he went balls deep into me, pulsing his hot seed straight down my throat. The moment he pulled out, I rolled onto my side, gasping, then yanked off the stupid mask for his sick slut fetish. This was worse than any of Noah's threats.

"That was so perfect," he spoke through heavy breaths. The caress he placed to my cheek was immediately slapped away. Shock etched his expression as he softly spoke. "Are you upset?" The bed dipped from his weight as he attempted to spoon me.

"You just used me like a crack-alley whore and called me a slut!"

"But that's just Kitty play." He kissed my shoulder. "You're not a slut." The soothing tone was more for a wailing child than for an adult.

My teeth bared, though, to no one. "I will never enjoy that." My choices were between a pillory or dying of asphyxiation by a cock. And who knew if Noah wouldn't put my mouth to equal torture. All this was permitted because of a stupid contract and a discarded ring.

At my demand, Jonah ran me a bubble bath and stayed out while I bathed. I spent what felt like thirty minutes washing the runny makeup from my eyes while I sulked in the bath. The need to immediately run away tormented me, but that seemed impossible. I had to get along with Jonah, or I risked Noah's intervention. But to be degraded as a slutty Kitty fetish didn't seem like anything I could tolerate any more than a pillory. I had to wonder how far I could push in my refusal to please Jonah.

For days, I refused Jonah's requests to put on the Kitty outfit. Those were days spent being wooed by him or, when he left, tormented by Noah. And his newest torment included having me collared and leashed at his side in one of the Kitty outfits of his choice with a jeweled plug lodged in my rear.

To humor himself, while eating dinner at the table, he had me seated at his feet one night awaiting Jonah's return from work. He'd also placed a tight, black mask over my entire head that only had holes for eyes, nose, and mouth. Cat ears adorned the top of the hideous second skin. It wasn't even meant to be attractive.

The expression on Jonah's face when he stepped in was indecipherable. I wasn't certain if he was shocked, angry, or pleased—he simply stood at the entry to the dining room.

I said nothing, given Noah had warned of gagging and flogging me if I did. Instead, my tormentor stroked my head as though I were a pet.

"This little kitty has been disobedient of your wishes." Noah's fingertips glided over my back. "I need to be training her."

Jonah's throat bobbed as he slowly walked our direction. "She's done nothing wrong to deserve that."

Noah huffed. "Do you like how well she behaves at my feet?"

Jonah took off his jacket as he sat on the seat behind me. "She won't even wear one of those plugs for me." He took advantage of the opportunity to touch me, his fingers migrating all the way down to my frilly black and white skirt. It looked how really skimpy maid lingerie might.

I hadn't worn any of it willingly.

"Get your cam. We're going to give kitty a nice shave." Noah's cold gaze shifted to me. "And she's going to behave."

Jonah scowled and muttered, "You shouldn't be touching her."

Noah stood. "And you should be, but you aren't."

Fear delved into my stomach. This was the moment the truth would come out. They were very communicative about everything but hadn't opened up about fucking me. What would they say? The only winner when things came out would be Noah.

"I fuck her plenty! Just not out here—yet."

The words I feared for Noah to discover spilled from Jonah in self-defense. Noah's glance down at me ended before I could look away. My mind raced at everything that might occur. Would Noah also share the details of what he'd done with me?

He didn't, not yet anyway. Instead, he handed the leash to Jonah. "Let's go to my shower and shave her so you can start slut-fucking her on cam." The words were meant as insults. Even the tone held ridicule. A new sort of shame overtook me at the way Noah spoke.

When they started up the stairs, I obediently remained at Jonah's side. It hadn't even taken any training, only a threat on Noah's part. I cringed at the sight of the now visible room that was a cage across from Noah's door. He'd been preparing it and taunting me about what he would do to me in there.

Once inside Noah's room, we went past the large bed he'd had me bent over on more than a few occasions. French doors at the far end of the room opened to the bathing quarters. They had a royal elegance and were larger than Jonah's. The gray-speckled marble was a refreshing cold against my palms and knees.

In the corner, Noah pulled a brass cord and water flowed down like rain from the cloud-white ceiling. After he felt the water for a few seconds, he called me over.

There was a smolder in his gaze as he slowly removed his suit jacket. His head bobbed to the flowing water. "Get in, *Slutty Kitty*," he ordered, rolling up the sleeves of his collared shirt. I couldn't understand why the words hurt coming from him, but they did.

Jonah knelt behind me and removed the white leather collar from my neck.

I wouldn't risk receiving further orders from Noah, so I crawled beneath the soft-flowing water and rolled onto my back where my head was between streams of the water, so none hit my face. My legs spread for his viewing pleasure.

"I left the kit downstairs," he said to Jonah as his gaze roved over my body. "Would you get it and the cam?"

Horror gripped my features; this would actually happen.

The size of Jonah's grin consumed my periphery. "Absolutely." I'd never seen him leave a room I was in so fast.

Noah set his shoes on the floor next to where his jacket lay. With the rest of his clothing still on, he came and dropped to his knees between my legs. For a moment, he only stared past the water that streamed from his hair onto my neck. He became drenched from shirt to feet, but he didn't seem to mind.

"So, you've been fucking Jonah?" Then his hands gripped my bare waist firmly.

My eyes widened. "No, no...I—"

"Don't lie." He leaned forward. "You have no idea what kind of punishment is in store for you once you're mine."

I didn't know whether to be terrified or excited. The uncertainty ended as he pushed my sopping skirt upward. "My cock isn't enough for you?"

"No...I mean yes..." I attempted to clarify. "It is enough." I scooted backward, but the tips of his fingers dug into my soft flesh as he pulled me into position beneath him.

Whatever he was about to say was interrupted by the beep of the bedroom door. He returned to an upright position and tucked his erection into his pants before lathering my legs with soap. I had no doubt he was seething, but what had he expected? That Jonah wouldn't attempt to touch me? The assumption had been absurd.

Jonah, dressed in nothing more than black house-pants, brought in a tripod that had a computer-screen sized monitor he snapped onto two of the legs. He placed it near the wall and attached the camera on top before handing the brown, leather shaving kit to Noah, who opened it and set the supplies outside the flow of water with precise care.

Jonah beamed to me as he clicked the long, brass cord to the shower so no more than sprinkles flowed onto me. The cold lather and tickle of Noah's brush caused a small twitch.

The screen turned on and showed me lying in the steamy sprinkle of water.

"Spread your legs toward the camera—Noah, move to the side, so we get a full view of her spread wide and being shaved." Jonah already sounded winded from excitement, and surprisingly in charge.

I let the image on the monitor guide my position, as well as Noah's angling me so the water didn't land on my face or where he would be shaving me. His movements were slow and precise, calming me from the gentle touch as I hoped his collected behavior wasn't truly resentment.

Guilt, for whatever unexplainable reason, I felt guilt, as though I'd stepped over an unforgivable line—and for Noah, of all people. The man who loved to torment me, who teased me and made cruel threats.

Jonah put on a brass wolf mask that covered the top half of his face.

Every glide of lather, swipe of blade, and stroke of fingers was erotic. It was Noah's perfected dedication and gentleness that made something so mundane into an experience I could have enjoyed if not for the shame I felt.

Even through steam, his blue eyes, set on perfection, melted me. Occasionally they flicked upward to meet mine, sending a tingle through me. I was uncertain what he was playing at when he pulled the blade back and traced his thumb over the side of my nub. Was this flirtation or cruelty? Each time he waited, tormenting me as my muscles relaxed again so he could clear another section with the blade.

Another set of blue eyes peeked through a predatory brass mask. Even the way Jonah's mouth gaped was new to me. He dropped his pants. The swollen erection bounced until he gripped and stroked it.

"She needs me to fuck her," Jonah said.

I didn't respond, but turned my face away from both of them. Private humiliation at the way Jonah would fuck me like a slut was far different from Noah or numerous others seeing. Marshal's accusations were coming true. Maybe it was my deflated response, but Noah stopped and patted my thigh. "Elbows and knees."

I rolled into position and spread wide so he could finish shaving me. Two naked feet came to stand in front of me. I tilted my head upward to Jonah, whose hand sped furiously up and down his cock. "You're so fucking sexy, Slutty Kitty."

Noah had finished the last few strokes and laid down his razor and begun trickling water to rinse me, but that was all. There was no torment. There was no hungry glance. There was only the sound of Jonah above me—most likely readying to publicly fuck my mouth.

I hadn't thought Noah's tormenting visits were something I looked forward to until they stopped. That only left me with Jonah, who'd been an annoyance I once believed kept me safe from Noah's dungeon and the pillory he warned me of.

But now, Jonah's fetish became my life. Playing Kitty might be tolerable if Noah was around making me feel unbelievably wild and whispering heart-churning threats of tormenting pleasure. But that time had passed.

I had no problem walking through the large house dressed as Kitty in hopes of spotting Noah, but it had been over a week since he discovered I'd been with Jonah. And that had felt like a month of role-playing Jonah's fetish, so he didn't pester me. A few times agreeing to let him webcam me as his Slutty Kitty. Even while I was on my period, he wanted me to suck his dick while on webcam.

When I finally saw Noah, I was standing at the kitchen island, tipping a fluke of champagne to my lips. He didn't notice the red and black skirt that bore a view of everything. Not even the cup-less matching bra or sparkly, red high heels. What he did notice was the cup of bourbon across from me.

I wanted to run and hide, to melt into the stainless-steel counters. But all I could do was tremble, feeling the waxy red lipstick against the glass. Champagne had never had a sound until that moment.

He passed me and went to the refrigerator, the rummaging also loud to my desperate ears that longed for his threats. But those threats never came. Maybe they would have had Jonah not returned wearing a suit and beaming at the sight of me. He loved wearing a suit while on cam; it made him look all the wealth he was while owning me. His grin flashed in Noah's direction.

Why hadn't my near nudity in front of Noah ever elicited a reaction? Perhaps it was the lack of attention given to me. Maybe if

Jonah had been at work, Noah's response would have been different. I had to wonder. It forced me to realize how I hadn't truly wanted to leave because I wanted Noah's attention. Be it his torment or the pleasure, he had kept me from never attempting to leave. For over a week, I felt like a pet who'd been disowned and waited hopelessly for forgiveness.

Jonah took a sip of bourbon, then asked, "Why aren't you on the table, Kitty?"

The refrigerator shut behind me.

My stomach felt as though rocks churned. I'd told Jonah several times I wouldn't have sex with him outside the room. He knew I wouldn't have obeyed his order to be waiting on the table.

I lowered my glass and circled around the island to go upstairs, stopped by the sight of his camera tucked in the corner of the room—the screen on, and me on it as I stopped.

"Why is this here?" I asked, glare on Jonah.

"Our viewers ask for me to take you and have my way with you somewhere new." His viewers, not ours. I would never claim them.

My horrified glance went to Noah's back as he poured himself a drink of a thick green liquid.

"Noah prefers watching people fuck. Don't get shy because he's in the room." Jonah sauntered toward me. The information left me curious, but my anger at Jonah had me nearly storming off for what he expected of me. But I didn't want to be outside Noah's presence. It had been so long, and he'd been on my mind.

"No," I snapped.

Jonah came closer, whispering. "It was hard getting Noah to come home to shave you. Please."

A gulp lodged in my dry throat. Noah was being forced to return. My actions had caused him to leave his own home? Was he staying with another woman? Tormenting her instead of me? What did it even mean that he preferred watching people fuck?

"Good little Slutty Kitty," Jonah spoke low against my shoulder. "But I have to punish you for standing in my presence." He stepped around and his arms wrapped around me, but not in a hug, my arms were locked to my sides as he turned me to face the camera then dragged me toward the table, causing me to lose a shoe in the process.

"Let me—" *go!* But I couldn't get the words out before Jonah pushed me against the table and rolled me onto my back. This would have been exciting if Noah had been the one holding me down.

"Noah, get the bindings on the cam." Jonah's hands loosened, and he whispered, "This is going to be so much fun, Kitty."

My eyes followed Noah as he strode to the camera setup and reached behind it to a coil of red ribbon. With a racing heart, I watched his steps as he drew near. But he was indifferent, not even casting me a single glance. I didn't want him to be so close while Jonah had his way with me. I struggled, my arms breaking free of Jonah.

Noah dropped the bindings, reached between me and Jonah, and captured my arms. "I'll hold her down while you bind her." The moment Jonah stepped backward, Noah was between my legs, only his soft house pants separating us.

For a moment, I stilled, craving this touch from Noah. But he wasn't doing this so he could torment me with pleasure. The press of his pelvis to mine revealed nothing more than a semi-hard cock. He was doing this so Jonah could live-stream mounting me. I squirmed beneath Noah's hold, wanting to either free myself or at least have him give that hungry, dominant look he used to give. Instead, his attention was on Jonah, who worked the silky fabric to secure my ankles to the legs of the table.

I raised my one free leg, attempting to roll over, my core rubbing against him. When his hold readjusted, one hand held both of my wrists, and the other gripped my free thigh, I froze at the touch. For the first time, our stares connected. The intensity brought an undeniable hitch to my chest that his attention shifted to.

He lowered my thigh, his open palm grazing upward, missing my slit as it continued upward, not slowing as it caressed my exposed breast and up all the way to wrap one of my wrists. He didn't need to lean forward, but he did anyway as he spread my arms into a Y. His length hardened a little more, but his gaze—only a foot away from mine—went to my hands, not me.

I hadn't even been aware of Jonah securing my leg until he rose, and my lower body could do nothing to get free. Noah stretched my arms tighter as Jonah secured a wrist to the side of the long table, then the other as well. The pull of my limbs was too tight for me to move anything but my hips or arch my back.

Noah stepped away, letting Jonah take position between my legs. "I'm going to punish my slut." He adjusted the mask on my face, which had tilted sideways.

Every time he called me that scathed me. Even if it was play. How dare he find such joy in my degradation. But when I turned my face, Noah was in view. That halted all thought. His cock was out, his hand stroking the length slowly. The flutter at the sight of him returned. Maybe once Jonah was gone—

Jonah pulled my jaw, so my eyes were on him as he thrust into me. Fingers went tight to my nipples, squeezing them with a pressure strong enough to force a whimper. The spread of my legs was wide enough, and his angle just right, that I couldn't stop the gasp of pleasure and arch of my back that his movements elicited. But the thing about being *Slutty Kitty* was that he got what he wanted, so it didn't take long before he was shooting seed into me.

As Jonah slammed as deep as possible and freed pulses of cum, he said, "Mewl for me, Slutty Little Kitty."

I didn't. Then he was done. There may have been a slight grin of approval he didn't let his audience see; I didn't know. I had opted to look past him.

He zipped up his pants. As he turned to leave, he said over his shoulder, "I'll get the shaving kit."

As soon as a beep came from an upstairs door, movement from my periphery had my attention set on Noah. The outline of his cock was visible from within his soft pants and made an impression as he stopped where I was bound at the edge of the table. He leaned forward so he braced his hands positioned at each side of my head. The familiar smell of him was intoxicating.

I leaned upward, hoping he would press his lips to mine, but he didn't lower his head.

"I thought you preferred being my slave to playing slut."

"I do." My response was more of a plea. A plea for him to treat me like his slave. To punish me. To torment me with unreleased pleasure and threaten the most cruel of things. I arched my back, wanting to feel his stomach against mine, and possibly welcome him to drop his body onto me.

"Then you would be in my dungeon, and not a little slut for a webcam." He used that word again. A name I despised, but maybe it was true. It didn't make me angry like when Marshal would call me a slut for the simplest of encounters with other men. It just hurt coming from Noah.

I sat on the edge of the bed and looked at my reflection in the wall mirror. The luxury silk sheet wrapped beneath my arms hid the thin camisole I wore. Jonah offered me more than I'd ever thought possible. When I was with Marshal, I fantasized about being the woman I read about in romance novels, or the female stars in movies with a man like Jonah. Kind and considerate, desperate for my smile. He should have been what I considered perfect, but I didn't.

He sat up behind me and kissed my shoulder, eyes peeking at mine in the mirror. I saw Noah when I saw those eyes. I hadn't seen him in a week, and it had been a rocky week with Jonah. I resolved to accept this time fulfilling the contract and accepted Noah wouldn't pursue me. Then I would leave, and I had made up my mind to leave Jonah once the time came.

"I have a surprise for Kitty. Will you play now?" Jonah asked, the smell of bourbon on his breath. This time, he'd had a bit more than usual. I knew he felt hurt that I avoided sex. Mostly because he thought he'd done something wrong.

My gaze shifted to the bathroom.

He gripped me by the hair at my nape, sending a rush through me and a hitch to my chest. Our stares connected again, and all I saw was Noah. "I didn't know you liked that," he purred, tightening his hand into a fist to pull slightly.

"Maybe a little," I breathed, tilting my head upward.

"I suppose I should have known, given how excited you were when I had you bound on the table last time." But Noah had been what excited me the last time. And this felt like him. He sat straighter, this time looking down at me with dominance. "Put on the outfit." The tone was one I had never heard from him.

"Yes…" I stopped myself from calling him Master. I wasn't sure if I liked being dominated, but I did love the reward of pleasing someone. Right now, that someone was Jonah.

I bolted to the closet, where he already had a Kitty outfit set out. It was a deep red with black spots in the design of leopard print. I put it on, admiring myself in the frilly silk skirt that ruffled and had black trim. It came down to barely hide my cunt, and the matching top pressed my breasts high. The garter had small bells inset in the front, red bows. And this time, the stockings were fishnet with small, sparkly beads.

After I placed the mask and applied a bold red lipstick, I returned to the room. Jonah wore a suit and leaned against a tall bedpost. One could assume he was posing for a photo shoot with his poise and the small glass of iced bourbon raised to his mouth. He tipped it to drink, then placed it on the cushioned top of the smaller cage at the foot of the bed.

My heart skipped a beat by the way he watched me walk to him in the black, knee-high stilettos he had chosen. He smiled, that dimpled smile that beamed his delight, then lifted a short, square box for me.

I hesitated, knowing whatever he gifted would be for me to play Kitty. I already second-guessed my willingness to don the outfit.

"Oh." He grinned. "I forgot; you want me to be more dominating." Those words reinforced that he had no understanding of how to be dominant.

After going to the bedside table and rummaging in a drawer, he came to me with a ball gag and held the straps so it dangled in front of my face. When my mouth opened in protest, he placed it and wrapped my head to cinch it closed. Oddly, it turned me on too much to back away. "Our viewers are going to love seeing you like this." As he spoke, he took the lid off the box and pulled out a black butt-plug that had a soft cattail. He pulled me against him and turned us, so my back was to the mirror before he reached down to find my tight hole and pressed the lubricated tip in.

I arched my back at the discomfort, pressing my stomach against his hard cock. I didn't stop him, though. There was something sexy about the semi-dominance and the smell of sweet bourbon on his breath as he placed a black collar on my neck.

He adjusted the tail to connect to the skirt, so it remained upward. Now the feeling of being a pet set in even more. "You like being my Slutty Kitty?"

When I had no choice, I did, aside from something shoved in my ass and being his Slutty Kitty. "Sure," I answered as a middle ground.

The bell on the collar jingled as he snapped a black leash onto it. "I want you on hands and knees."

I obeyed, looking ahead to see his reflection as he stared down at me hungrily.

He reached backward to his glass and took another drink. "Once I start fucking this perfect pussy, that bell isn't going to stop ringing." He stepped around me and tugged the leash. Obediently, I crawled beside him, feeling the same heat as when Noah had ordered me to do so. We left the room, and I saw the camera at the far end of the hall near Noah's room. It faced our direction with the screen already showing our slow approach. To the right, I noticed the wall had been opened to the room with tall bars. The cage room Noah had threatened me with. Jonah pressed a button that lit it from within. I got a view of its dim lower level that reached to hip height.

Previously, it appeared more like a jail cell, but now it looked like a cage for a pet to wait in. A white carpeted human-sized cat tree for climbing while on hands and knees had been added against the other side of the bars. It led to the lit upper area above my viewing ability from where I crawled.

I slowed, and the short leash tugged at the collar, jiggling the bell.

"Kitty," Jonah chided. He reached down and grabbed the cat tail and pulled, angling the plug uncomfortably, so I had to move forward. Shock etched my expression when I studied the screen that showed me on webcam. The gag made me look the part of a slave, and when I studied him not wearing his mask, I could see a morph of his charm mixed with Noah's demanding presence.

"That's right, Kitty, you've been bad." A motor hummed as several bars beside me raised to knee height. He pulled sideways on the tail toward the entry. "Get in so I can punish you." At his slurred, slightly stern tone and the firm pressure in my ass, I whimpered and obeyed.

Once inside, the bars hummed as they lowered into place. I turned to him and waited, looking up to his groin that swelled, then upward to the clank of ice as he lowered the glass to his chest.

"On this pedestal with your ass to me." He pointed to the highest square that was at his thigh level. As I approached the steps, he angled the camera setup.

One by one, I climbed them until my hands landed on a soft, green shag carpet. He went all out on making it look like a yard at this height with the sky-blue paint aside from a large white rectangle in the wall straight ahead. The image of my cunt and the butt plug projected onto it.

"Spread your legs." Jonah reached in to capture my thighs as I spread them. He pulled back until my booted legs extended out and knees were on the edge of the pedestal and ass was to the bars.

Words popped up at the bottom of the projection.

Yank her tail up.

Spank her.

"They already love your punishment, Slutty Kitty."

I whimpered into the gag as he pulled upward on the tail. The camera zoomed as his fingers teased my slit. I couldn't deny the excitement of seeing what his fingers were doing as they spread my folds to my glistening entrance and nub, thumb stroking either side of it.

Fuck Im cumming already.

Finger fuck the wet slut.

More viewer names and chats continued to pop up on the projection.

Jonah's fingers sank into me, slow at first, then curled at the tips and began pumping into me. His hand came down hard on my ass, jingling the bells on the garter and leaving a red mark extending out from the frill of the lingerie skirt. His uncoordinated hands were rough.

"God, I have to fuck my bad little slut." His fingers lowered, and I heard his zipper as a small camera on a post rose from the green carpet about five feet in front of me. The projection switched to my face looking forward and Jonah behind me looking like the handsome millionaire that he was. The pedestal my knees were on rose several inches.

Squeeze her tits.

"Take off your bra, Kitty. And watch me fuck you."

I obeyed, awkwardly unclasping the back and letting it fall to the carpet as I looked ahead.

Jonah's fingers dug into my waist as he slammed his long cock into me. Every bell jangled and my breasts bounced with his hard thrusts. All the while, vulgar viewers made their demands of what would be done to me. He reached in and pulled my collar, causing me to arch my back and giving a better view of my breasts.

My fingernails dug into the carpeting, and my knees burned from the friction with every pump as he fucked me through the bars of the cage. I whimpered and moaned at the pain-laced pleasure, my eyes fluttering as the bliss increased.

I can't wait until that cumming whore is pregnant.

Jonah unclasped the gag and let it fall, knocking my mask crooked over my brow. "Mewl for me." He spoke through heavy breaths and wiped sweat-dampened hair from his brow.

My moans came out choppy at the rapid thrusts as I screamed my release. The walls within me clenched tight around his girth while he continued to ram me into a non-stop oblivion. The man must have been suffering whiskey dick.

A sturdy yank to the collar had my back raised and arched against the bars. His blue eyes in the projection seemed to rove over my full-frontal view until his massive hands cupped my breasts and his thumbs harshly pressed to pinch my nipples.

I groaned as my hands curled around the bars above my head for support. I watched his length extended from his suit pants and pumping in and out of me. The darkness in his eyes and the way he touched me brought back those moments of torment with Noah.

"I can't wait until these are bursting with milk. You want my baby, don't you?" By the momentum, he was close to orgasm. Right now, sweaty and achy, pleasured and pained, all I could do was look at the man owning my body and want him to have all of me.

"Yes, Mas—" I stopped myself from calling him Master.

*Call him Master, slut...Knock the cunt up...*The chats continued to come onto the screen, each more vulgar than the previous.

With a hip-jolting thrust upward, his cock went hilt-deep. My hands squeezed the bars as he rammed me upward. Blasts of warm seed shot into me as he breathed onto my shoulder. He didn't pull out, but let his hands wrap over mine as he caught his breath.

He hummed against my neck as his lips trailed it. "I'm going to jack off at work to the sight of you in this cage."

Given Jonah's soft nature, I didn't expect him to leave me. After he zipped his pants and the projection of us shut off, he kissed my back. "I'll be back later."

I turned and reached through the bars to grab his sleeve. "Jonah!"

He smiled and readjusted the mask that hung crooked on my forehead. The dominant facade was already a memory. "Noah will let you out for a break."

I licked my lips, still tense at Jonah's decision to leave me in this cage, but I'd see Noah. "Noah? He's coming home?"

"Of course. I'll see you later, Kitty." He leaned in and kissed me, a soft kiss. Only traces of the bourbon remained on his lips.

As I found my red leopard print bra and put it on, my mind reeled at the thought of seeing Noah again. He was coming home, and Jonah wouldn't be here to interrupt the man I craved. Everything could be explained away. I would tell him I preferred him. Even if it started the contract time over. He would have to understand that I had no choice but to have sex with Jonah. I did as was expected.

Had I known the dungeon was a choice meant for me to make on my own, I'd have taken it without hesitation. I would have chosen him. Not that I didn't like Jonah. The gentler brother had been kind, but I wanted him when he acted dominant—when he acted more like Noah. Maybe Noah also could show the softer side that I sometimes enjoyed in Jonah.

My excitement turned to anxiety as the hours passed. I stood in the upper level and began to pace, biting my nails. Noah wanted me. Even though he didn't try to fuck me when Jonah left me bound to the table, he had wanted me.

Eventually, I slumped by the bars, squeezing them as I watched down the hall toward the stairs. By the time I did hear movement downstairs, I was desperate to pee. Even then, he didn't come up. The smell of garlic and peppers wafted up, bringing a rumble to my empty stomach. Had it been Jonah, I would have called and demanded to be let out, but this was Noah and his game of torment. A torment I missed.

Anticipation had my heart fluttering. It had gone silent for too long after the sounds of cooking had stopped. Once my head dipped at the cold abandonment I felt, I heard the soft steps up the stairs. Then I saw him stepping into the hall, rolling up the left sleeve of his blue dress shirt.

He said something, but not to me. Then a woman ascended. Jaimie from his club. The one who'd brought me outfits. He'd been spending his time with her. Cooking for her.

My unwanted swallow caught in my throat. The visual he must have loved seeing as my adam's apple bobbed with my uncertainty.

Without a glance at me, he pushed the button on the wall, and the bars of the door at the lower level hummed open. I wouldn't go. I turned my back to the bars, unwilling to let him see the pain.

"As soon as I'm done with Jonah's slutty little Kitty."

If only I could claw my ears out at her giggled response. I didn't want to know what he would be doing with her as soon as he was done with me. My stomach ached with the weight inside. I'd wanted him. I still wanted him. Even seeing him with her, I wanted him to choose me. But I wouldn't say that. He would refuse me whatever I wanted. And maybe this was just a game of his.

His voice deepened. "Out, Slutty Kitty."

For several seconds, I remained seated with my back to him. Maybe he truly did think me a slut unworthy of being trained by him.

His fingertips tickled up my spine, teasing me with touch and igniting my skin with delight. A delight magnified when he pulled the collar so the back of my head came to the bars. "Now."

Tingles filled me, sending desperation between my legs. Combined was the humiliation of submitting to him in front of the woman who stood at his side. This was an act, nothing more. Torment. He wanted me to feel this way. She'd even brought me clothes that she knew he would like. She didn't want him for herself. At least that's what I had to remind myself of.

I looked up to her for a sign, but she behaved as though I wasn't there, focusing her adoring eyes on Noah. Maybe he brought her here to upset me. She didn't need training.

He turned toward his door as I rose. "Come to my room in an hour." He spoke over his shoulder as he led Jaimie through his door. There was no pulling me close, no warm breath rolling over my face, no promises of torment. He was gone.

I rushed to soak in a mound of coconut scented bubbles, not concerning myself with going to Noah's room or filling my empty stomach. My mind wouldn't stop whirling with all the excuses of why Noah brought Jaimie with him. The game he played to cause me to react. But all too soon, I had to make sure he wasn't using the hour he had demanded to fuck her.

My hands trembled with the anxiety of seeing them alone. Every moment had the buzzing in my nerves increasing until my body felt like a hive of bees lurked within. I jerked on my short, red silk robe. Even my feet crackled with energy as they carried me down the dimmed hall toward his door.

Soft light trickled out from where it sat ajar, but I could see no one. I slid it further open. No beep announced my arrival, so I slipped in. The amber glow of erotic lighting made the firm ridges of his shoulders and torso more appealing. The shadows made his rigid expression more dominating. But that strength wasn't on display for me.

I had been wrong. And despite everything inside telling me to turn and run, I remained on unsteady feet, watching as Noah leaned against the post of his bed looking down as his broad hands tangled in Jaimie's hair. She knelt on the floor with her wrists bound behind her back.

The sight had me uncertain what to do. My stare met his. She made a gagging sound as his defined body rocked forward. I shouldn't have felt jealousy. Sadness shouldn't have swirled with the anger that burned within me. But they all landed with a blow that had my jittery hand bracing against the wall.

The moment I snapped from the shock of it and realized I could leave, he ordered, "Stay, Slutty Kitty." The dominating tone was one I'd succumbed to on numerous occasions.

My back planted against the wall. Waves boomed in my ears in the rhythm of my heartbeat.

"Up," he ordered Jaimie, who rose gracefully despite her hands being bound behind her back.

She said nothing as she obeyed a silent request and got onto the bed. She positioned on her knees while facing the direction I stood. Her cheek and shoulders lowered to the mattress and her back arched, so her ass angled upward to accept Noah.

He ripped a condom wrapper with his teeth and tossed it to the floor. As he rolled the latex over his massive erection, his eyes tilted upward to me as he got onto his knees on the bed and grabbed her hips. He slammed into her. The bastard held in place and moaned. "Good girl," he purred, "Let Jonah's Slutty Kitty learn from how good you are."

It felt as though he took his time, wanting me to hear the forceful slaps and animalistic noises they both made. I couldn't watch, but I couldn't look away either. This woman stayed there and took it, whether he rammed deep, pounded fast, or jerked her hips back to take his length. She seemed to love every damned minute of it. And she got it. *She* got to have him.

"Be my audience and watch me fuck my slut, Kitty," he demanded.

I wanted to refuse, but I also wanted to please the man whose gaze smoldered with lust. We watched each other as he pounded into her fast and hard. I hated how it turned me on and infuriated me. I detested how I wished I was the woman beneath him. If he were claiming my body, he wouldn't even bother with a condom. He never bothered wrapping his cock when he fucked me. But I couldn't gloat. Jaimie was the one getting to fuck him.

I'd been so caught up on Noah, Jaimie didn't even seem real to me until I heard her moan. Another rush of desire had my thighs rubbing at the sensation between my legs.

Noah bowed forward, hips jolting as he moaned his release into Jaimie. He quickly unbound her hands then immediately pulled out and threw the condom on the floor next to the wrapper and another condom he must have used on her before I arrived.

Me and Jaimie waited unmoving as he went to the bathroom and started the shower.

"Sluts," he called, and both of us rushed his direction. At my realization of answering to the name, I stopped outside the doors and looked in. The water flowed down Noah's sculpted body. I wanted nothing more than to be right there with him, rubbing the jasmine soap over my skin. I looked to see where Jaimie had gone, and she was near the wall angling the camera and monitor that were off.

Would he further torment me with his cruel games? I spun to leave, but before I could rush from Noah's room, a wet hand captured my arm.

"Your master wants your cunt shaved." The words were spoken close to my ear, but not whispered.

"You aren't my master," I snapped, yanking my arm free.

"I'm not. I'm simply doing as he requested." He gripped both my arms, but not hard, as he steered me toward the shower. "And look, Jaimie's going to wear her slutty bunny ears and help out. I bet you didn't know you're both pets." His words were laced with sarcasm.

I glanced at Jaimie, who beamed at me from where she stood by the camera. She seemed delighted as she placed a headband with black bunny ears. The ruffled, black lingerie skirt she put on hid nothing from sight. Once she checked the mirror and smoothed her hair, she turned on the camera and pranced in front of it.

"You know how we do this, Slutty Kitty." Noah stood out of the camera's view, holding the leather cat mask that would fully cover my face. His stance made me certain he wouldn't accept my refusal.

I went to him to take the mask. Instead of letting me put it on myself, he grabbed my sash and pulled me against him.

"You liked standing by and watching me fuck a slutty webcam pet, didn't you?"

I didn't look up into the oceanic eyes glaring downward. If I had, all strength would have faltered. He would have seen how much his actions had affected me, so I lied. "Yes." I breathed deep before adding, "Master."

He pulled the sash, so the robe cracked open. Ever-so-slowly, he roved a hand up to my breast to cup it. With his other hand gripping my ass, he growled low into my ear. "You only think being my slut would be fun." He squeezed, bringing me to whimper.

All I wanted to do was remain close to Noah, to take in the smell of his skin and feel his breath on my shoulder. To enjoy the firm grip he still held to my rear. To feel his cock grow hard and know he ached for me. But all I got was him working the tight black mask over my face and tucking my hair beneath it.

I rose to the tips of my toes to whisper, "Please." There were too many requests I wanted to make. I wasn't sure which I was asking, nor which one he believed I asked.

The sensual feel of his hands gliding over my shoulders had my core ache with intense desperation that had me rub against him. His touch tickled past my shoulders and pushed the silk robe down to pool at my feet. Now our eyes did connect, further creating a desire to be fucked by him. The man may have already spilled his seed twice, but his dick began to swell against my stomach.

My eyes closed to await his kiss. Once his warm mouth was to mine, I opened to welcome his tongue to dance with mine. The brief connection had me wrap my hands over his shoulders to pull him in for more.

He broke away, a glare to his expression. "Be a good little pet for Jonah and lay down in front of the camera and don't move."

At his cold refusal, I went to lay in front of the camera on the warm tile beneath the slow-dripping, steamy water.

"There's something I want to do before he shaves you," Jaimie said.

"My fans are watching too, so just lay there or I'll have Noah give me a gag and flogger and flog the hell out of you." Jaimie's dominant growl surprised me. She was supposed to behave as submissive as she had with Noah, yet something in her expression suggested she would flog me to the point I might show the marks for a few months. Her presence at that moment held equal command as Raven, but the bunny facade returned, and she cast me a joyous smile as she knelt at my side and nudged my knees, so my legs butterflied and rested against the floor. Her palm followed my thigh up to my slit.

I jolted, but her fingernails dug into my dampened flesh. The darkness in her expression warned me to obey. Something about the situation had me willing, maybe just to prove I hadn't been bothered by what I'd seen her do with Noah. Maybe in hopes to see his excitement and possibility that he would respond to me.

"Good girl," she whispered. "You have a pretty kitty, Slutty Kitty."

I scowled, though the mask probably didn't allow for my expression to be made out.

She pinched my nub, causing me to flinch, but I didn't dare make a sound. The pinch softened, but she kept those fingers to both sides of the sensitive bundle of nerves, tugging and stroking. Although the feel excited me, it still wasn't Noah's touch.

I glanced up to watch him swirl a shaving brush in a bowl while watching Jaimie expose my cunt. I could make out the line of his erection in the black pants he wore, but he didn't pull it out in excitement.

She leaned forward and pressed her soft lips to my nipple. The pads of my fingers pressed to the slick tile as I tried not to respond too much to the way her tongue flicked over the pebbled peak as her fingers slithered into my cunt.

Through it all, my gaze lingered on Noah, whose jaw clenched, and chest swelled with deeper breaths. He didn't take his eyes off me when he placed the shaving bowl on the floor.

The excitement of being watched enhanced the sensation of her skilled touch that had my hips slowly rocking. She slowed, letting my nipple free before turning her attention to the other. The sight had Noah's eyes occasionally flicking up to mine. The intensity of his interest sent even more desire through me, bringing my body to a new level of ecstasy. He liked this. Sure, he was still angry, but he enjoyed watching me.

Jaimie switched to slapping my nub several times, then alternated to swirling her fingers over it. Her teeth claimed my nipple, bringing my back to arch as her fingers slithered into me and curled in a sensation that had me biting my lip as I kept my focus on the handsome man in the room.

His lips were slightly open in a way I'd seen several times when he craved my body. Just the sight of that want in his eyes had my walls tightening. For a moment, I imagined Noah's seed shooting onto me instead of the drips of warm water. I imagined him coming over to have his way with me.

When Jaimie's face rose, she looked between Noah and me before she pushed my cheek to face upward at her malicious smile. "Noah has chosen me, so stay out of my way."

Her declaration caused my heart to sink. He chose her. What had he said to make her so certain? She'd told me on the first meeting that he never trained anyone. But how had he chosen her? As his slave to train or as someone to fuck? He rejected me before I lay down in the shower to be shaved. It wasn't truly me that he found interest in, he simply loved watching people. I was no longer of interest to him. The day couldn't get any worse as every hurt and angry emotion slammed into me. At least I thought so until Jonah stepped into the doorway and went straight to Noah.

"Jaimie was supposed to help as you shaved Kitty, now everyone's demanding more of this," Jonah hissed.

Noah shrugged with indifference to the situation. "Two sluts are better than one. You've already received 1K for the performance."

That didn't seem like enough for how angry I felt at Noah. For the lies. But he hadn't lied. He'd outright rejected me then let Jaimie play her game for profit. At least he claimed it was about profit.

I glowered at Noah. This had been set up intentionally. Assuming their options for my work only included a camera, I would be stuck with Jaimie for months due to his anger. He had found a new way to torment me. His expression suggested he knew exactly what I figured out. Would he also spend that time fucking her and making me watch in hopes of hurting me further?

Even though I wanted to seethe, it would only bring tears. I wouldn't let him see that his actions had affected me. Not for a single second would he get that satisfaction.

Jonah jerked off his suit jacket and tossed it onto the floor, then relocated the camera for a side view. After he marched over to tower between my legs and yank his large cock from his unfastened pants, he said, "Turn up the water. I want my Slutty Kitty in the fucking rain. God, you're so fucking sexy." Jonah dropped to his knees and rapidly pulled my legs over his shoulders, so my backside lifted from the tile. The lighting lowered, and water streamed, and when I looked to the screen, it did appear as though Jonah slammed into me beneath a rainy sky with a realistic looking outdoor backdrop of a forest.

Jaimie's face lowered, and she used the tips of her fingers to force me to look up at her sly smirk hovering inches from my face; another warning flashed for me to behave. When she lowered to kiss me, I turned my face away to continue my scathing stare at Noah. Fuck her and her arrogance and fuck him and his dickish games.

"This slutty slave has been bad. Can we punish her?" Jaimie asked Jonah.

"Fuck yes," he hammered deeper, rocking upward to rub against the spot within me in a way he knew I loved.

Jaimie crawled forward until her bare cunt was inches above my face, blocking the pour of water, but worrying me of what else she may have in store. I considered ending the event, but Jonah's grip on my thighs tightened. Not to mention, I wouldn't let Noah win this battle.

It had to be Jaimie who pinched my nipples so painfully I cried out, my back arching as something clamped them.

"God, that is so sexy," Jonah said. Why was he so close to this woman? He supposedly held interest in me, yet wanted to be so close to her nude body. I still held strong, unwilling to show any emotion Noah was attempting to elicit. He must have been waiting, he had to be desiring me, but he also must have hated seeing Jonah have me.

A similar pain from my nipples went to my nub as something clamped it as well. The ache had my hips thrust upward, giving Jonah a better angle to fuck me with more speed than I would have thought possible.

The bitch above me giggled, seeming all too pleased by my humiliation. The thought of Noah fueled my want to continue. It was no longer about wanting him to want me beyond the fact that my acceptance hadn't been part of his plan.

After her satisfaction with causing me discomfort, Jaimie stood, giving me the chance to turn my face to the camera. Why did I want to see the events occurring? I had no clue. Certainly not to look at the sight of short, black clips on my breasts and nub. The one barely visible at my nub was quickly blocked as Jaimie stepped forward and gripped Jonah's soaked, dark hair.

"Eat my cunt," she ordered him before curling her hand to the back of his head and pulling it tight to her. The woman must have loved forcing me to watch her do that. Noah had chosen her, but she got Jonah, too.

The sight of his eager hands gliding up her wet thighs had me all the more furious. No, I'd never wanted him as much as I had wanted Noah, but I also didn't want to see this. The man who'd been so kind and behaved as though I was the only woman he wanted only needed a camera and another person willing to play pet to prove otherwise.

Stepping into my view next to the camera, Noah had the look of villainous satisfaction. I had no idea what expression my face held; I didn't bother to look. It may have been a mix of pain and pleasure by the way Jonah's cock still had my body in a state that craved release as he continued his thrusts. Maybe that infuriated me as well, the way he could still pleasure me while doing the same to another woman he seemed to already know how to please.

Within moments, Noah sauntered over, keeping his back to the camera, but not blocking the view of my body. The only sound remained the water and Jaimie's moans of pleasure in response to Jonah. Noah lowered onto his elbows and whispered close to my ear, "I think you should ask Jaimie to be the one to train you. She's a good Dom for webcam sluts."

My teeth bared at him calling me a slut. "I hate you," I growled low. I despised him for fucking Jaimie in front of me, but for forcing this emotional pain upon me, I absolutely hated him.

"No, you crave for me to bring you more pain and pleasure than anyone else ever could."

But he was wrong. He had to be wrong. "I crave nothing from you."

"No? You would have already climaxed if I were the one inside you." Noah's head moved over one of my aching nipples. He removed the clip and gently brushed his lips over it, exhaling warm air over the throbbing peak.

The moment his lips touched down, my traitorous body responded and rocked upward to press against his mouth for more.

Jonah responded to the movement, pistoning in and out of my drenched cunt. So much pleasure hit me in all the right spots, not to mention the irrational desire for more of Noah's touch. Adding his hands and low moans, he brought me to hover on the precipice of bliss, causing me to move against him for more, sometimes teasing and pulling back until I had to take a deep breath of air for my breast to reach his warm lips.

It wasn't Jonah's rapid pumps that sent me into orgasm, but Noah's gentle caresses and attention to my breasts. I despised him even more for being able to do this to me.

The clamping of my walls around Jonah set off a chain reaction of him beginning to pound into me. The intensity must have also been present in his tongue by the way Jaimie's moans grew into cries of pleasure.

"I don't want to block your view of Jonah pleasuring another slutty pet," Noah whispered as he re-clamped my breasts and backed away as Jonah and Jaimie orgasmed at the same time.

It didn't seem possible that Noah's secret could remain when viewers would be messaging about the other man whose face they couldn't see but was obviously doing something to me. Then how would he explain his actions to Jonah? Maybe he wanted his brother to see. They might both decide to share Jaimie as their pet instead of Jonah keeping me as his *Kitty*.

After Noah shaved me, he and Jaimie stayed in his room. My stomach ached and gurgled from hunger after at least fourteen hours without food. I struggled to yank off the mask as I rushed to Jonah's room. Ignoring him, I donned his long, cotton robe before storming past where he stood in my path to the doorway. He reached for my arm, but I didn't let him stop me. This past day and most of the night had been an absolute nightmare that started with him fucking me in a cage and ended with him cumming inside me while he ate Jaimie's cunt with a vigor that made her cum.

Forget what Noah had done. That was torment enough. I'd always thought Jonah was the considerate one. Annoyingly needy, but genuinely desired a relationship with me. What they'd both done had crushed me. I didn't even think I would care what Jonah might do with another woman, yet I did. And the fact it was Jaimie, who'd threatened me and fucked Noah in front of me, made it worse.

Jonah followed behind as I rushed down the stairs. "Don't be mad. It just happened."

"That didn't just happen. You knew she would be here." I continued past the spacious dining and living rooms to the kitchen.

"I didn't want Noah to shave you without someone else here, and I wanted to experience you on cam from afar...Lizzie, please," he pleaded as he caught up behind me.

I whirled. "You don't call me Lizzie. Call me whatever the fuck you want, but don't call me Lizzie." He had no right to give me a pet name aside from calling me his slut, and I wouldn't let him. I turned again and went to the pantry.

"Let me cook something for you."

"No." As soon as I said the word, my stomach growled. "How much longer until my contract is up?"

"We were on cam; it won't happen again. Don't leave over one mistake?" Without answering the question.

I took the peanut butter and bread. It was a comfort food, one that my mother made me on my worst days. I had to step around him, bundling the items in one hand as I went to the fridge for strawberry jelly. "One mistake? Is that what you call how long you locked me in a cage? Or letting her do what she wanted to me? Or fucking worshiping her cunt?" I slammed the food down on the counter. When I reached for a spreading knife, he took one from the drawer and handed it to me.

"Noah was supposed to come soon after I left." He shook his head. "She was supposed to be there for your comfort." His firm body pressed to my back as he braced his hands to the counter at my sides.

I elbowed him in the arm as I made my PBJ.

He winced and stepped backward. But despite my actions and feelings, I wanted him to stay, to be like Noah and not let me fight or argue. Was it even Jonah who upset me? No, and it wasn't Jonah who'd ripped my heart out, but it was Jonah who let me vent. And I had every right. If he hadn't kidnapped me with the excuse of a stupid contract, I wouldn't have to endure any of this.

"You need someone to order you around, just like Jaimie did. Why don't you make her play as your slutty pet and fuck her, so I don't have to be your stupid Kitty?"

He went to the bar and pulled out a glass and bourbon. A long sigh escaped as he strode to the counter to stand across from me on the dining room side of the counter.

I finished making my sandwich and took a large bite, glaring at the bottle as he poured. Maybe he would drink it, then demand I not argue. It was the only time he attempted to dominate me. Instead, he sat on a stool and spun the glass.

Perhaps the silence was him giving up. I could take my opportunity to go back upstairs, but that would require I pass him. Would he stop me? Could I pass and go into the room to start a bath? He could have his few drinks and gain the courage to make demands. But why would I want him to be like Noah, who'd fucked Jaimie in front of me? The thought had me bent forward with inexplicable tears falling to the counter. This shouldn't have been so complicated.

Why did I even care about Noah? Why couldn't I be satisfied with someone like Jonah? Were my expectations too high? Why couldn't there be a middle ground between the two? One person who would be loyal to me. But I was no different in how I enjoyed fucking the brothers. Maybe I deserved it. No, there was no maybe. I did deserve it. I didn't deserve happiness at all.

"Elizabeth, please." For once, he called me by my name, not that it made me feel any better. More bourbon poured into the glass. "Give me another chance. You don't have to play Kitty, and I don't want anyone but you." He reached to my chin to lift it to look upon his somber face. "You're wonderful to me."

Something about his expression melted me, and if I had to choose between the twins, I had to choose Jonah. Noah wouldn't be forgiven.

· · · ·

JONAH SPENT THE NEXT hour comforting me with a cooked meal and simple conversation about some of his joys. It was the first time he shared much about himself, but I enjoyed the distraction so long as Noah wasn't mentioned.

After a few glasses of champagne, I enjoyed learning that he was saving the amount of money from our time camming. Six thousand dollars. All of it would be mine, but he promised to buy me anything I wanted, anyway.

We were both slightly drunk when we were in bed and he pulled up the information from the webcam earlier. That one encounter had accrued two thousand dollars, half of it mine. But as he read the chat stream, he glanced over at me, a bit deflated.

"You let Noah touch you to get even with me for what I did with Jaimie." He wasn't angry with me, at least he didn't appear to be. At the time, I wouldn't have minded him suffering the sting of knowing about Noah and me, but every time his sweet side returned, I didn't want to hurt him. Just like his brother, Jonah could have my heart swinging like a yo-yo.

I didn't respond to the statement.

"I'm sorry," he softly said and leaned over to kiss me before the room darkened.

I wasn't in love with him, but I still felt bad for his hurt, even more for the way he felt like he had been in the wrong. I'd always wondered why Noah kept our sexual actions secret, but now it seemed obvious. He didn't want to hurt his brother, and at every step had attempted to figure out a way to take me for himself. From the first night when he demanded me to reject Jonah and through all his taunts to get me to do something that would force him to oversee my training. He protected Jonah.

My own guilt had me whispering my sincere apology for his hurt feelings. Though it wasn't an apology for the undeniable attraction I had to Noah's dominant personality that kept me on my toes. Even now, I wished I didn't feel the secret desire for him. I wished I could hate him without a hint of desire for his touch, but that would probably never happen despite my greatest efforts.

My head ached when I woke. Fortunately, it wasn't a full on hangover. I downed a glass of water and donned my short, black robe. A familiar beep at the door should have notified Jonah that I was leaving the room, but he was passed out. By the timing, the beep must have been Noah's doing. Most likely his way of knowing everyone's movements in his home. It had always worked in his favor in the past.

I padded down the stairs toward the kitchen, slowing at the noise of someone in the room. The sight of Noah's muscular back as he stood on the far side caused a hitch to my breath.

A moment of uncertainty consumed me. I could simply return to Jonah's room without acknowledging Noah. That would be the wiser choice, and he didn't deserve to see me. I couldn't hide from him forever, though, not when he lived here and came and went as he pleased.

The need to alleviate the residual throb in my head nudged me onward for something hydrating. Opting not to hide from him, I continued with silent steps toward the refrigerator. I could pretend we were roommates who rarely spoke. He knew either me or Jonah would be down given the tone on the bedroom door that went off.

After choosing fruit punch, I turned to make my way to get a glass. Noah had already taken position in front of the cabinet I needed. He leaned against the counter with his arms crossed high on his bare chest and bore a glower that would frighten a bear. My next deep breath didn't give me the courage to approach him for a cup. With all resolve faltered, I decided to return to the room and use one of the small glasses from the bar.

"Women make him nervous. It's the only time he drinks," Noah said from behind me, shutting a cabinet. "And he hasn't shown interest in a woman for years."

I wasn't certain how to respond. I was the cause for Jonah's drinking? I supposed he would have a glass he barely sipped from when we first met, but drank a bit more often now.

"Here you come, everything a lovesick puppy could want, and getting him drunk for your own comfort. Letting his infatuation swell to a point of no return. Women like you..." Instead of finishing his statement, he huffed. There were numerous possibilities of what he could have said. None would have been compliments. And maybe I would have deserved it. More than ever, Jonah was my way of staying away from Noah. I didn't want to hurt Jonah, though.

"Stop fucking with my brother's head, or I'll share some details of things you like and make him a special dungeon to keep you in." His accusation and threat were infuriating.

They kept me here. I hadn't come willingly. Jonah was a captor, and Noah was a bastard who wanted to toy with my emotions?

"So I could play Kitty in a pillory? You seem to forget that I didn't choose to be here, and I don't want to be here." Fear melted my feet to the spot as he stood and marched to tower so close I had to tip my head upward to meet his stunning gaze.

I shouldn't want him. I shouldn't want him.

I shouldn't want him! The mantra played in my mind, yet I waited with bated breath.

"If you don't want to be here, the fucking door is over there." He flung an arm out and pointed toward the entry. "I'll have a car at the ready for you whenever you choose."

My step backward ended in a stumble to hit my lower back on the adjacent counter. I hadn't expected him to say that. Did I want that? I should. It was what I looked forward to. To be away from Jonah and end the torment Noah subjected me to.

His eyes narrowed at my momentary reverie. "But you have nowhere to go but back to my Ark to begin your forty days of slut training."

The word fueled my own rage. Everything he'd done made him the bad guy. But why deny being called a slut when I could cut deeper? I stood straighter, refusing to cower even if he had me cornered. "I didn't take you for the jealous sort."

"Jealous? You think I'm jealous my brother fucks you like a piece of meat for thousands of people to see." Too close; he stepped too close so I could smell the intoxicating sandalwood. "Streamed at my work? Everyone hearing what a slut you are? That's my face everyone sees just as much as it is his. And he hasn't bothered covering it recently."

My heart sank. Noah watched every time Jonah had me on cam. And it wasn't that Jonah was fucking me, but Noah's own embarrassment that people might see him fucking me. If I'd had anything in my stomach, I would have vomited it up at the immediate disgust. What hadn't I done to be ashamed of myself? A few times, my mask had come loose.

I wouldn't back down. Not to the man who'd fucked another woman in front of me because he knew it hurt me. "I'm okay for you to fuck so long as no one knows! You're so proud of Jaimie that you probably fuck her on a stage." No other words came in my anger and hurt. Staying to be degraded any worse was not something I could handle. My escape failed from the tight grip on my upper arm. Of course, he wouldn't let me leave so easily with the final word.

"I'm Jonah's slut, not yours, so let go of me."

But he didn't let go.

"Is that why you slipped up and almost called him Master?" He yanked the tie of my sash, letting it fall to our bare feet. "It was me you wanted when you practically begged to be knocked up." Ungentle hands spread the front of my robe and groped me before rising to fist my hair and yank my head, so I looked up to him. There were no spoken orders, yet he was more in control than ever. "I'll give you what you want." The worst part was that I wanted this. I wanted his seed to pulse inside me. I craved his touch. Even if I didn't already have an IUD, I wouldn't shy from the risk. The ache in my head was no more than a distant throb, but my mouth watered and my cunt leaked.

Without any warning, his cock slammed into me. Any whimper of shock and pleasure drowned in the firm kiss that claimed my mouth. I received what I hated, but had been so desperate to have. The passion that had been buried returned in full force and had me tipped backward, lifted only by the arm wrapped tight around my ass to contain me as his pistoning went balls deep. He pounded with a force I'd never felt before, but every thrust felt so deep it pierced my soul.

My fingernails dug into his rigid shoulder as hot blasts of seed coated my walls. For a while, he remained lodged deep in me, brutally claiming my mouth in a kiss.

He stepped back and left me feeling empty as his cock left my drenched cunt. After a few deep breaths, he said, "I'm sure Jonah's waiting for his slutty Kitty."

"And Jaimie's waiting for her prick." But I knew the truth. I could have chosen the dungeon Noah often threatened me with, but I'd found refuge with Jonah's calm demeanor.

"Why the fuck would I want a pet?" Fury ignited in Noah's features before he grabbed me at the waist with a bruising grip. "I would have had so much fun breaking you."

My eyes widened with a desire for more of what only he could provide.

His next thrust of his still-hard cock had my rear sliding onto the counter. Even more unbridled as he had me with impassioned ferocity. So opposite from the man who maintained absolute control over himself and me.

He didn't slow down and tease my body or bark the order for me to orgasm. It happened on its own. It happened without his focus on my pleasure. By the end of his next climax, we both were panting through the way our mouths fought for dominance. If ever there was a man to have me completely, it was him.

But when he stepped back and quickly readjusted his pants, every one of those ecstatic thoughts I'd had came shattering down. He was leaving without so much as a threat and forceful kiss. I wouldn't be waiting for the torment I hated and loved after he fucked me.

Almost a week passed since my last encounter with Noah, but it was one that had my mind reeling for him. The forty days were almost up. In the entire time, Jonah had only been kind and hadn't mentioned the incident with Noah while on webcam. It was painful to know Jonah thought he'd done something wrong, but the truth would hurt worse.

I'd become lost in my reverie when the bubbles in my bath swayed around me. I removed the soft mask from my eyes and looked ahead, offering a warm smile at the sight of Jonah.

"Turn around." His blue eyes glistened.

I turned and rested my elbows on the flat edge of the tub. I should have loved the way he brought a loofah to scrub my back. I should have loved everything about him, but I couldn't. Even when the water flowed down my skin, and Jonah kissed my shoulder the way only his lips could, my thoughts clung to Noah.

Jonah inhaled deeply. "You smell good enough to eat."

"You just ate," I retorted. I had to wonder how many women felt the same way I did. A life of privilege they felt trapped in with a deserving man they couldn't love but also couldn't hurt. Somewhere along the way, I had foolishly fallen for Noah's torment. And his piercing blue eyes didn't burn passionately for me, at least not anymore.

Jonah hummed against my spine as he spoke. "But not you, yet." His gentle scrub went along my arm, curling around to glide over my stomach. There was a long silence as he soaped me, paying attention to every detail of my upper body.

Tickles trailed my ear as he whispered, "I love you so much, Lizzie."

I could smell the bourbon. We hadn't been playing Kitty and Master on cam, not since the encounter with Jaimie. And he hadn't attempted to assert dominance, which he only ever mastered after a few drinks. I began to understand what Noah meant by me causing Jonah to drink. It wasn't intentional. I wasn't trying to get him to drink, but it was the only time I had ever accepted him.

A heaviness filled my stomach.

"You've known me hardly over a month." I scooted to the side.

"And I've loved you at least half of that." He ran the loofah down my left arm.

"You shouldn't." My response was a bit bitter. This was what Noah had feared would happen. Jonah would be hurt by me. Jonah had refused to grow attached to a woman because of women like me leading him on. "I don't deserve someone as caring as you."

It wasn't a lie. This man and his kindness deserved so much more than me. Sure, he had used a contract to keep me captive, and he had his fetishes, but in recent days I refused, he left the subject, choosing to do something else. Sometimes something as simple as offering a walk. I always paid attention on those walks, because the consideration of sneaking away still hovered in the back of my mind.

"Can't you just accept being loved instead of trying to resist it?"

I glanced at his glazed stare, then to the sudsy water he squeezed from the loofah before he rubbed it along my neck. All I could do was nod. "Sure."

"Good. Come to bed and make love to me." He got out, bubbles streaming down his toned abs and legs. After helping me out, he didn't even bother with a towel before the quick trip to the bed.

The sex was indescribable, with a dedication to my needs that knew no bounds. But that was Jonah. Outside of acting out his Kitty fetish, he was a passionate man. He was giving and never bossy. And he loved me. A love unrequited, and that I didn't deserve.

I waited after the glow of our orgasms and for Jonah to slumber. The whole time thinking about how I would leave. There was a time I would have stayed and waited to receive money from him, but I didn't deserve it. I also didn't want to lead him on for months. I hadn't formed a plan in all the time I'd been here because—even though I refused to admit it—I knew this was where I'd wanted to be. But now, it was the worst place for me to be, for Jonah's sake.

I'd leave a note to explain myself. His immaculate room didn't have a single pen laid out, so I went to my closet for an eyeliner pencil. Rummaging through for paper only led me to a gift box he'd recently given me. The pink and silver stripes on the outside of the box made it a perfect card. I ripped the thick edges of the thin cardboard and folded it into the size of a note card.

Inside, I wrote, *I'm so sorry, but I'm too broken to love you the way you deserve. Thank you so much for being wonderful, Elizabeth.*

Simple words that told the truth, along with countless lies. The coward's way out, but the only way I could do it.

After taking several minutes to compose myself, I got the one pair of athletic shoes Jonah had gotten me for our recent walks. Given I had no good outerwear that was warm enough for night, I opted for his sleep pants and one of his long-sleeve shirts. With a towel wrapped around everything I would put on, I made to find my way out.

I couldn't leave out the front door though. That might set off an alarm. The balcony wouldn't set off any alarms and wouldn't make a sound since Noah wasn't here. More resolved than I thought possible, I took Jonah's key and snuck out the balcony door.

Now for the hard part. Padding through the chill night air over to Noah's side of the balcony, every inch of my body filled with dread. This was the only way down. After dropping the towel with my clothing to fall beside the shimmery pool that glowed brightly in the darkness, I found a perfect spot to climb onto the balustrade. For a while, I stared down, attempting to gain courage to land in the frigid water. It was going to be the sort of cold that felt like knives, and I was about to dive in. A few minutes to build courage wasn't too much to ask of myself.

Tormenting moments passed as I considered going back, but staying wasn't fair to Jonah.

With another deep breath, I let go.

Blades, unimaginable shock to my skin. How could water be so cold in comparison to the air temperature? Even when I crashed in with Jonah, it didn't feel this icy. Now it felt like a tormenting eternity before I surfaced. And that gasp of air had me coughing as I breathed in some of the water. Even the few strokes I swam to reach the edge felt like a nightmarish challenge.

My shaky hands could hardly grip the ladder, but I managed to pull myself up. My teeth chattered as I rushed to the towel that had my clothes strewn near it. Warmth couldn't come fast enough as I dried off. It must have been in the upper fifties, which isn't bad with long pants and long sleeves, but wet and naked, it was terrible.

I found the pants instantly and put them on. The shirt was next to a pillar a few feet away, with my shoes near it. I kept the towel wrapped over my shoulders as I scurried over to the rest of my clothing.

A tall silhouette stepped from around the pillar. How had he known and gotten here? I stepped backward, heel trembling on the concrete that felt as though it had turned slippery.

Noah POV

My little slave looked up to me with scared eyes—the same eyes she had when she didn't know what I planned to do to her that first night at my club. But her face wasn't filled with enough terror. If she knew what was in store for her, those knees wouldn't be trembling from the cold. They would be buckling from fear.

She glanced up at Jonah's balcony. Letting her remain with him would be detrimental to both of them. Dominance wasn't in his nature, and she found refuge in submission.

"Jonah has no say in this." I prowled toward her; she'd already backed to the edge of the pool. There was nowhere she could go. "But I'll have fun making you the perfect woman you poisoned him into believing you were." Not that I had any intention of sharing her again.

I wanted so badly to bend her over and claim her body, but my cock was a reward she would have to earn. It took every bit of my willpower to stop myself.

"Just—just let me go home." Beyond her cold trembles, she didn't move as my chest pressed against her. "I don't want this job you tricked me into signing a contract for."

"You think this ever had anything to do with a contract? You aren't leaving." I tangled my fingers into her hair at the nape of her neck, silently ordering her to look up at me. "Not in forty days, not in three months after that—" My fist tightened in the tangles "—not ever." She wouldn't want to after I was done with her. All she would want to do is obey my every order and melt into the caresses I would reward her with. I would have to shatter her first.

Don't miss out!

Visit the website below and you can sign up to receive emails whenever Maebel Credence publishes a new book. There's no charge and no obligation.

https://books2read.com/r/B-A-SJRX-JHKQC

BOOKS 2 READ

Connecting independent readers to independent writers.

Also by Maebel Credence

The Heir
Dominated by the Heir

Standalone
Armon's Revenge
Neighborly Attraction
Noah's Ark

www.ingramcontent.com/pod-product-compliance
Lightning Source LLC
Chambersburg PA
CBHW072011150726

47999CB00002B/610